How To Keep a Partnership Professional

Steve Miller Says:

1. Let her know you don't believe a woman belongs on the police force.

2. Try to get her to quit by exposing her rookie inexperience.

3. Pretend your dog is the "significant woman" in your life.

4. Don't fall in love with her warm brown eyes, lustrous hair and incredibly sexy intelligence.

Liz Casey Says:

1. Give him a traffic citation for speeding.

2. Show him up by outshooting him at the target range.

3. Pretend your cat is the "perfect man" in your life.

4. Don't fall in love with his sexy grin, lean build and irresistibly self-assured nature.

Dear Reader,

I got a speeding ticket once. Okay, okay, I've gotten speeding tickets twice. Unfortunately, neither ticket turned into a romance with the cop who stopped me. All I ended up with was a court date (much less fun than a dinner date, I promise you) and a fine. Author Patricia Hagan clearly has better things in mind for her characters, though. Pick up *Groom on the Run* and you'll see what I mean. Because when policewoman Liz Casey stops Steve Miller for speeding, all sorts of interesting and exciting things ensue. Like sparks, like romance…and like a very difficult working relationship when she discovers *he's* a cop, too. Pretty soon you can forget misdemeanor speeding and go straight to love in the first degree!

You'll love our second book for the month, too—Marie Ferrarella's *Cowboys Are for Loving.* This is the second in her miniseries THE CUTLERS OF THE SHADY LADY RANCH. Kent Cutler is a cowboy through and through, and he's flat-out not interested in having any city girls hanging around the ranch. Although there's something about Brianne Gainsborough that…well, as you'll see, even the toughest cowboy can be roped and tied when the right woman comes along.

Enjoy them both, and rejoin us next month for two more Yours Truly novels, books where Mr. Right is just around the corner.

Yours,

[signature]

Leslie J. Wainger
Executive Senior Editor

Please address questions and book requests to:
Silhouette Reader Service
U.S.: 3010 Walden Ave., P.O. Box 1325, Buffalo, NY 14269
Canadian: P.O. Box 609, Fort Erie, Ont. L2A 5X3

PATRICIA HAGAN

Groom on the Run

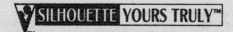

Published by Silhouette Books
America's Publisher of Contemporary Romance

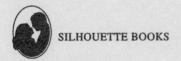

SILHOUETTE BOOKS

ISBN 0-373-52076-X

GROOM ON THE RUN

Dear Reader,

I am so pleased to bring to you the zany, warm and wonderful story of police detectives Liz Casey and Steve Miller. As partners on the force, they must battle crime…as well as the heated emotions that surge between them.

Steve had been romantically involved with his last partner in California. When she was tragically killed in the line of duty, he vowed never to work with another woman. Liz does not know the reason for his hostility but is determined to succeed in her career. And though conflicts abound, they are ultimately, helplessly, drawn into each other's arms.

Groom on the Run, my thirty-third published book, was such fun to write, especially since I have a nephew on the police force in Birmingham, Alabama, the setting for Liz and Steve's adventures and romance. The research and planning were so interesting and fun, and I hope you enjoy reading their story as much as I enjoyed writing it.

All my books are a pleasure for me to create here on a mountaintop in western North Carolina. I fall in love with my heroes, feel the emotions of my heroines, and I ultimately weep with joy when all ends well and happily.

Happy reading!

Patricia Hagan

1

It had been one of those days, and Liz Casey, Birmingham city cop, wished she had called in sick that morning and then pulled the covers over her head. Filling in for someone who was truly ill, however, had kept her from being able to do so.

Rain had been coming down steadily since she'd gone on duty at seven that morning. The streets were slick, which meant more than the usual number of fender benders and wrecks. She despised them because of all the paperwork involved. Every line on a wreck report had to be filled out in detail because of insurance. Then, too, there was always the chance of it winding up in court, and cases had been won or lost based on what the officer had written.

Liz also didn't like having to deal with the drivers and passengers involved in a wreck. Tempers sometimes flared, and on more than one occasion she'd had to break up a fight—which had just happened at the accident scene she'd just left. A little old lady in tennis shoes, who had been rear-ended by a socialite in high heels, had whacked the socialite over the head with her umbrella. The only reason the socialite didn't take out a warrant for assault was that Liz had assured her she would have to spend an entire day in a busy, crowded court in the company of wife beaters and drunk drivers.

Despite her rain cape, Liz had gotten soaked in the process due to the whipping wind. Working fast so tow trucks could clear the area and get traffic flowing again, there had been no way she could have handled an umbrella while taking notes and measuring skid marks.

She had just gotten back in the dry comfort of the patrol car and was making final notations to her report when she heard her car number called over the radio.

Snapping her book shut, she sighed and lifted the mike. It was 2:45, and she hoped she wouldn't be sent on another call so close to the end of her shift.

"Car thirty-two," she said woodenly.

"Wreck on Sixteenth Street, near K-Mart," Carl Bundy, the dispatcher, reeled off the information. "Three cars involved. No injuries reported. Big fender bender, though. Get to it."

"Wait a minute, Bundy. I go off duty in fifteen—no, thirteen minutes," she corrected herself as she glanced at her watch. With the day she'd just had, every minute counted. "That location is at least five minutes from here, and I wouldn't have time to write up the report. Besides, I've got to head in to the station to turn in my paperwork, anyway."

"Oh, you'll have lots of time for that, Casey. The sergeant just assigned you to pull another four hours."

Liz hit the steering wheel with her free hand and yelped in protest, "He can't do that."

"He can...and he did."

"But why? I'm not even supposed to be working traffic, remember? I'm patrol division. I only agreed to help out Batson because she had a root canal yesterday and feels like she got run over by a Mack truck, and—"

"No whining," Bundy said with a chuckle. "That's the first rule of a good traffic cop, Casey."

"I am *not* a traffic cop," Liz bit out the declaration. "I just told you—I'm standing in, and—"

"Yeah, yeah, I know."

Liz heard a noisy slurping sound and knew Bundy was pulling on a straw, which meant he was enjoying a thick milk shake. Other cops might cover their desks with framed pictures of their kids. Not Bundy. He wanted the space for the junk food he was forever consuming.

"But did you remind the sergeant of that fact? I shouldn't be expected to pull overtime."

"Maybe not—" he paused to slurp again "—but maybe you do need to be reminded that you don't want to make any waves just now, what with you asking for a promotion, and—"

"Me asking to be promoted to detective from patrol should not have a darn thing to do with whether or not I puddle around in the rain for four more hours, Bundy. Now, I've served my time out here in hell, and—"

"And you'd best be getting over to that wreck, Casey, 'cause I've got another call coming in from that area, and I'll bet a doughnut it's somebody raising hell 'cause you ain't there yet."

She felt like telling him she'd never be fool enough to take such a bet. Bundy would never wager a doughnut lightly.

"All right. I'm on my way. But lighten up, will you? I haven't even had a break since lunch."

"Tell it to the nuts out there running into each other." He chuckled and, with another slurp, clicked off.

"This is what I get for doing a favor," Liz groused as she weaved in and out of the heavy traffic, then felt guilty. Carol Batson was a good friend who would do the same for her if called upon. Besides, it wasn't Carol's fault that having her appendix out six months earlier had used up all her sick leave. Financially, she couldn't afford to lose a day's pay, so Liz had agreed to fill in for her. The force didn't care, as long as her beat was covered, and it had been an off day for Liz, anyway.

"Why can't people just stay home in bad weather?" Liz grumbled to herself. In her opinion, if they weren't on their way to or from work, or in the midst of a life-threatening emergency, they shouldn't be out. Kids didn't have to be hauled around in a monsoon, and women could miss a day at the mall without having their world come to an end, and—

Liz gave herself a vicious shake and gripped the steering wheel tighter.

She had to stop being such a sourpuss. She hadn't always been that way, for there had been a time, not so long ago, when she had taken everything in stride and didn't let anything get her down.

But that, she frowned to think, had been B.C.—Before Craig—because being married to Craig Stover had taken the sunshine out of her life, to be sure, and she had to get over it.

Getting over *him,* however, had not been a problem. She had already done that before she'd finally left him. Packing her bags less than a year after they were married, she had walked out and never looked back.

Craig hadn't wasted any time finding a replacement, either. Three months later he was married again, this time, Liz heard, to the quintessential Stepford wife who catered to his every whim.

Reaching the congested area of Five Points, Liz was forced to come to a stop. A minivan had slowed for a red light without pulling over to let her go by in the passing lane. The blue lights on top of the cruiser were already flashing, but Liz also switched on the siren to make the driver notice and get out of her way.

The woman at the wheel of the minivan merely glanced at her in the rearview mirror with a bored expression.

Liz eased closer and turned the siren louder.

The woman shrugged and gestured to the steady flow of cars crossing the intersection.

Liz pointed for her to move toward the curb so she would have room to get by.

The woman pretended not to understand.

Hemmed in, Liz could only sit there and wait for the light to change. Any other time she would have gotten out and written the woman a ticket for deliberately blocking an emergency vehicle, but it was pouring down rain. She would have to puddle around in it soon enough and decided a few more minutes delay would not matter. Bundy had said there were no injuries at the scene, which meant she would only have to deal with irate drivers and passengers.

Drumming her fingers on the dash, Liz shut out the sound of the police band as she allowed her mind to wander back to that period in her life she now blamed for her crabby attitude.

Craig Stover had been, for all outer appearances, the ideal man. Nice looking, clean-cut, well dressed, Liz had met him when she was a rookie cop assigned to the downtown beat. He had been in his last year of law school at the University of Alabama.

That day, Alabama had played Auburn at Birmingham's Legion Field and won, and Craig and some of his fraternity brothers were celebrating. They had gotten a bit rowdy at a local bar and grill. The owner had become nervous and called the police, and Liz had been the one to investigate the complaint.

The disturbance hadn't started out to be serious—just

some shouting back and forth between Craig and his friends and some Auburn University stalwarts. By the time Liz arrived, however, things had escalated beyond name calling and might have been about to get out of hand, but she was able to quickly impress upon them that she would haul them all to jail if they didn't cool it.

Everyone backed off and started leaving.

Liz assured the owner she would be in the vicinity should he need her again and turned to go—only to find a Tom Cruise look-alike waiting with a big, flirty grin on his face.

Craig had proceeded to boldly introduce himself, said he was from Mobile, and would she please let him buy her dinner when she got off work, because he thought she was the sexiest cop he'd ever seen and wasn't about to let her walk out of his life.

Liz had immediately fallen under his spell, fool that she was, and not because she was inexperienced with men. Far from it. She'd had a few relationships, the memories of which kept her warm on a cold winter night, but right then there was no one special in her life. After all, she had been busy the past two years getting her associate degree in law enforcement, and, just starting on the force, there had been little time for romance. Besides, she had high ambitions, and marriage wouldn't be on her agenda for many years.

So, in retrospect, Liz could see how she had been ripe for someone like Craig, because she was burned out from studying and training, and hungry for some tender R & R— recreation and romance.

She was twenty years old and had missed a lot of good times, and Craig showed her a whole new world—frat parties at the University of Alabama, football games, weekend trips when she could arrange her schedule to be off.

They had met in November. By Christmas she was in love—or thought so, anyway. Easter, he took her to Mobile to meet his parents, and in June, right after he graduated from law school, they were married.

Then the trouble began.

Craig went to work for a prominent law firm in Birmingham at a starting salary that was four times more than what she made as a rookie. For a wedding gift, his wealthy parents gave them a house in a ritzy neighborhood, and he wanted her to stay home and take care of it. But Liz could not bear the thought of doing nothing but keeping house. She told him that it would be different later, when there were children. For the time being, she wanted the career she'd worked so hard to get.

But Craig had been adamant, insisting it was extremely important to *his* career for them to have an active social life. That meant golf and civic clubs for him and junior league and bridge games for Liz.

What it didn't mean was her continuing to be a policewoman—a job, Craig felt, unfit for his wife.

It had been on their honeymoon—a Caribbean cruise, a gift from Craig's rich grandmother—that he had shown his true colors and told her how he felt.

Liz had been furious that he hadn't issued his ultimatums before the ceremony. She also reminded him of how he'd claimed that her being a cop was one of the reasons he'd been attracted to her.

But Craig had no remorse or shame when he admitted that dating a policewoman had merely been a lark at the time. Furthermore, he said, she should have had sense enough to know that he, as a lawyer on his way up the ladder of success, would not want his wife to work around criminals, for heaven's sake.

He had also told her how proud she should be to have made such a catch by landing him as a husband. He offered a life of wealth, leisure and social acceptance—while she, foolishly, sought a career he considered beneath his class.

So they had walked up the gangplank of the ship hand in hand with stars in their eyes but left a week later, tight-lipped and angry.

Craig had continued to constantly nag at her to quit her job, while Liz kept trying to make him understand how she felt. She reminded him how she was a fourth-generation police officer but wanted more than to merely walk a beat. It was her ambition to move up to patrol, then detective.

But Craig hadn't understood, and the wall between them became higher with each passing day.

The light changed.

A horn blew behind her.

Liz was jolted back to the present and felt like a fool for being in a trance with blue lights whirling and siren wailing.

Once more weaving in and out of traffic, she soon reached the latest fender bender. As Bundy had reported, there were no injuries, but there his accuracy had ended. Instead of three cars, there were four, which meant a longer report had to be made.

Rain was coming down in sheets, and it was impossible to take notes without having the paper get soaked. In the other wrecks, she had managed to hold her rain cape over the clipboard, but the wind was blowing so hard the cape whipped all about her.

It took nearly an hour and a half to get all the statements she needed, take measurements and have wreckers clear the scene.

As water ran down her nose to drip off the end, Liz thought of her friend and muttered, "Paybacks are hell, Batson," then reminded herself once more to stop being such a grouch.

No sooner had she finished than Bundy dispatched her to another wreck, this one on the interstate.

"That's state trooper jurisdiction," she protested. "Not city."

"Sorry, but the stretch where it happened is inside the limits, and it's a big one. The troopers asked for city backup to direct traffic. Hop to it, Casey. You've got over two hours left on your shift."

Bundy sounded as if he was enjoying himself, and Liz decided he had to be a closet sadist who got his kicks delivering bad news.

She clicked off, not about to give him the satisfaction of hearing her whine further.

The rain was not letting up. Liz didn't even bother wearing her cape when she got out to direct traffic around the eight-car pileup. At least it was warm for October. Otherwise, she would probably have wound up with a cold, maybe severe enough to put her in the hospital, which, at the moment, didn't seem like a bad thing.

But, despite the temperature, which was probably in the eighties, she began to shiver and sneeze. Every stitch she had on was soaked. Still, she was no better off than any of the other officers puddling around.

"You should have been born with webbed feet, Casey," one of the troopers teased. "You look good wet."

Liz pretended indignity. "Hey, watch it, Davenport, or I'll claim sexual harassment."

He laughed. "Nothing sexual about saying you remind me of a duck, Casey."

She gave him a mock glare and returned to waving at agitated motorists to hurry up and drive on by. She thought how most people did not stop to realize that the traffic backups at the majority of wreck scenes were not caused by the wreck itself, but by drivers curiously slowing down to see what had happened.

At last it was over. The wreckers pulled away, and traffic began to flow smoothly. Since she didn't have to do any paperwork, Liz hurried to the cruiser.

She glanced at her watch. It was nearly seven o'clock. She punched the mike. "Car thirty-two to base. I'm going ten-eight."

Bundy came right back at her. "Aw, Casey, don't you want to take one more call? I've got a great one for you over on Pine and Third. A car hit a light pole, and—"

"Pass it to somebody else, Bundy. I'm out of here."

Liz released the mike before he could argue. All she had to do was take the car to Carol's precinct, grab a bus to her apartment, and the night was hers. Hot bath, jammies and robe, phone for a pizza, then curl up on the sofa in front of the TV with Tom.

Liz smiled to herself.

It all sounded terribly cozy…except for one thing.

Tom was a cat.

He had deposited himself at her back door during an ice storm back in January. She had invited him in for warmth and a meal, and evidently he liked the accommodations, because he had become a permanent resident.

She was almost at Carol's precinct when Bundy's gloating voice came over the radio again.

"You gotta report in, Casey. The sergeant wants to see you."

Liz punched the button and groaned, "And you've gotta be kidding. Do you know how wet I am? How hungry? And I'll have to bum a ride from somebody to get there. My car is in the garage, and if I have to wait for a bus in all this traffic, I could be midnight getting there."

Bundy chuckled. "You're wasting your tears on me, Casey. All I do is deliver the messages."

He clicked off, but not before she heard the slurp of another milk shake.

How long were his shifts, she wondered, agitated. If the truth were known, he probably worked for nothing if it meant he could be the harbinger of bad news.

Liz knew there was no point in trying to talk herself out of her bad mood. Stress management said to consider such a day as a learning experience, but enough already.

She reached for the switch to signal a left turn but realized it was no longer working and wondered what else was going to happen before the wretched day finally came to an end.

"Well, at least the rain has let up," she mumbled, rolling down the window to give a hand signal.

And that was when she found out the next misery on her agenda, because just then a little red sports car went whizzing by, hitting a puddle to send a spray of muddy water right into her face.

"That does it," she growled, hitting the siren and doing a frenzied U-turn in the middle of the street.

Radar said the driver was only doing thirty in a twenty-five-mile zone. Ordinarily she would have let him go, but muddy water in her face was as good as a slap after the day she'd had.

At least she wouldn't have to chase him down. The driver pulled over immediately.

Liz slid to a stop directly behind.

She got out of the patrol car and slammed the door. Mud and water streaking her face, she walked to the driver's window and, without preliminaries, coldly snapped, "Driver's license and registration."

"Look, Officer," came the voice from inside the car, soft

and cajoling, "I was only five miles or so over the limit, and—"

She cut him off. "Then you knew you were speeding."

"Yes, but I'm late for an appointment, and—"

"And that's no excuse. I'm late, too, but you don't see me roaring around on rain-slick streets."

She couldn't see his face but could hear the sneer in his voice as he retorted, "That wasn't exactly a slow and easy U-turn you just made in that intersection."

"It was justified." She held out her hand. "Have you got a driver's license and registration?"

"Yes, I do, but I was hoping you'd give me a break. You see, I'm an officer, too—a detective. Here, I can show you my shield and ID."

Resentment flashed through her. A detective. Something *she* longed to be. And here he was, driving around all nice and dry splashing water on her.

"Then that's all the more reason you shouldn't be speeding."

"Hey, can't you give a fellow officer a break?"

"No. You set a bad example. You've no business racing around in this kind of weather, splattering water all over people, and—"

"So that's what this is all about." He leaned out of the window, then, to glare at her. "I accidentally hit a puddle and spray you, so you're going to bust me for going five miles over the limit. Thanks a lot."

Liz thought he might have been really attractive if it hadn't been for the way he was scowling. He looked to be in his late twenties, with dark, thick hair and green eyes fringed with lashes too long and thick to belong to a man. He was well built, too. She could tell by the way his white shirt stretched across his wide chest and by the strong cords of his arms that showed beneath his rolled-up sleeves.

"I am late for an appointment at my precinct," he said slowly, evenly. "Surely you can understand that, officer. Don't you sometimes get called in for a meeting?"

"Yeah," she said with a sniff. "Like right now, in fact, and you're holding me up. So if you don't hand over your license and registration, I'm going to have to assume you don't have either, and—"

"All right, all right." He threw up his hands. "I know the routine. But it seems to me you could bend a little for five lousy miles. Hell, I'll even pay to have your uniform cleaned and throw in a trip to the beauty parlor if it'll make you happy."

"You don't need to make me happy." Liz was having a really hard time controlling her temper. "You just need to show me your license and registration, like I've asked for twice now, so I can write you a ticket."

He leaned across the seat and opened the glove compartment.

Under his breath he said something that sounded like, "Women cops...always got to throw their weight around."

Liz felt her spine go rigid. "What did you say?"

"Nothing." He shoved the papers at her.

"Yes, you did. You made a snotty remark about women cops."

"And so what if I did? You can't arrest me for that. So just write your ticket to make your quota for the day, so I can get out of here."

He was glaring up at her again, and, despite the anger sparking between them, Liz still could not help thinking how attractive he was. Under different circumstances...

She gave her head a vicious shake and took out her ticket book from her hip pocket and began to write. She saw by his license that his name was Steve Miller.

"I've had a bad day," he mumbled.

"So have I, Detective Miller," Liz mumbled right back. He chuckled. "I can tell."

She tore off the ticket and dropped it in his lap. "Five miles over won't give you points against your license, but they accumulate, you know."

"I'll remember that next time I pass a cop, but if it's a woman, and she's had a bad day, I'll probably get pulled over, anyway."

Liz couldn't help laughing, and, hands on her hips, looked down at him in wonder and said, "You really do have an attitude, don't you?"

"And so do you, but at least we won't have to worry about clashing at work."

"Because I'm traffic, and you're detective, right?" She smirked to think he was reminding her she was lowest on the police department's food chain.

"No," he said innocently. "We're in different precincts. You're in Second, and I'm in First."

Liz bit back a groan. First was her regular precinct. Filling in for Carol had put her in Second, which he thought was her regular beat. But why, she wondered, hadn't she seen him around before? Not only was he drop-dead gorgeous and would have been the whispered talk of all the female cops on the prowl for a man, but she also knew each and every one of the detectives, out of a longing to be one, herself.

"How long have you been there?" she asked.

"Just started a couple of days ago."

"As a detective?"

"Yeah. I worked for the LAPD in California, so it was fairly easy to get on here."

Again, Liz fought to keep from groaning. There had only been one opening in the Detective Bureau. Steve Miller being hired meant she had been passed over. And it wasn't fair, she thought, biting her lip. She was qualified, had all the necessary classroom instruction, had passed all the preliminary exams, and, by rights, the opening should have been filled within the department rather than by a sort of transfer. But strings were pulled sometimes, and procedures were bypassed, and there was no need to protest and make waves. That would only result in making her superiors think twice about promoting her the next time there was an opening.

"Well, thanks for nothing," he called sarcastically as she walked away.

She turned long enough to flash her most impudent grin. "You're very welcome, sir."

Back in the patrol car, Liz watched as the sports car eased from the curb and back into the flow of traffic, then pounded the steering wheel with her fists. "This, Liz Casey," she admonished herself, "is the reason you go home every night to a cat—because you act like you've got PMS all month long, darn it."

She drove on to Second Precinct, parked the car and turned in the keys, along with the accident reports and the lone speeding ticket issued to Steve Miller. After that, she had the first bright moment all day when a patrol officer going off duty offered to drop her at her home station.

Finally, with a sigh of relief, Liz took the steps two at a time, pushed open the precinct doors and announced to the desk sergeant, "I'm here, and whatever it is, make it quick. I've never wanted a day to end as badly as this one."

He pointed to a door. "The big Kahuna himself wants to see you."

She stared at the sign proclaiming the office of precinct commander and grimaced to think he was only now getting around to telling her she had not made detective.

Shoulders slumped, Liz went to the door, knocked, and called softly, "Officer Casey, sir."

"Come in," he responded.

She was surprised to see he was grinning and wondered if he was secretly related to Bundy, the closet masochist. "You wanted to see me, sir?"

"I did. And it was important enough to keep a pot roast waiting, and if you knew what a good cook my wife is, you'd appreciate that." He stood and held out his hand to her. "Congratulations, *Detective* Casey."

Liz felt as though she'd swallowed her gum, even though she wasn't chewing any. Thrilled, as well as stunned, she gasped, "But I heard the opening had been filled."

"We had two," he explained as he sat back down and motioned for her to also have a seat. "One came up suddenly. You know Joe Fisher, don't you? Well, he decided to take early retirement when he had a little heart attack last month. His wife insisted. You must not have seen it posted on the board."

"No, I didn't." Her head was spinning as she tried to grasp the wonder of it all, that she had, at last, made it. She was going to be a detective. She would have a gold shield and felt like shouting it to the world. Instead, she swallowed hard and fought to sound cool and professional as she said, "Thank you, sir. Thank you very much. I'm honored."

"Ah, you deserve it." He glanced at his watch. "Your new partner was here to meet you almost an hour ago, but you weren't here so I told him to go have supper. If you don't want to hang around, you can meet him later—"

There was a sharp knock.

The commander called to come in.

The door opened, and Liz blinked, hoping against hope that the man walking in was there for another reason.

Hope quickly died, however, when the commander heartily announced, "Detective Casey, meet your partner—Detective Steve Miller."

2

Walt Rogan, Chief of Detectives at Birmingham's First
Precinct, stared at Steve Miller through templed fingers. He
was leaning back in his chair, feet propped on his desk.

Steve was sweating as he waited for the chief's decision
on his request for a different partner.

Finally, with a sigh, Walt Rogan lowered his hands from
his face and asked, "Did you say anything about this to
the precinct commander last night because he introduced
you to Liz Casey?"

"No, sir. I thought it would be best to come straight to
you. And if I may say so," he added, "I was surprised he
told her instead of you."

"Ordinarily, I would have, but he wanted to break the
news to her himself. He regards her very highly—as we all
do," Rogan was careful to emphasize.

Steve was trying hard to keep a pleasant expression on
his face, when he was boiling mad inside. "I can appreciate
that, sir, and I assure you my hesitation here is objective—
not subjective. You see, the fact is, I just don't want a
female partner."

"No," Rogan said matter-of-factly, "the fact is—it
doesn't matter what you want. You need a partner. So does
Casey. You're an experienced detective. She isn't. You can
help her."

Steve felt as if his insides had turned to rubber bands, pulled tight and ready to snap any second. "It seems to me that we should both be assigned to veteran detectives. After all, I've only been here a few days, and you placed me with Mulvaney. We were working well together. Why pull me off and stick two rookies together?"

"Because you aren't a rookie. You've got a lot of experience with the LAPD. Nine years, in fact."

"And I've taken the last six months off. I'm rusty."

Rogan laughed. "No, you aren't, and you know it."

"Well, I'm not familiar with procedures here."

"You were given a manual your first day. Read it."

"You haven't said why I can't stay with Mulvaney."

"Mulvaney," Rogan explained, "has a partner, remember? Larry Spicer. He's been on maternity leave, and now he's ready to come back to work. He and Mulvaney have been together a long time. They're a good team. I'm not about to break them up. The truth is, you just don't want to work with a woman. And it's funny—" he pointed to a folder on his desk "—I can't find a thing in your confidential records that even hints at you being sexist."

Steve fought the impulse to pound his fist on the desk. "I'm *not* sexist. I just don't happen to think a woman should be a detective. It's too dangerous."

"All police work can be dangerous. We had a meter maid get run over by a drunk driver a couple of years ago."

Steve threw himself back against the chair. "I don't like it, Rogan, and, quite frankly, if I'd known I'd be paired with a woman I never would have taken this job. I would've stayed in California." He knew he sounded like a petulant child but couldn't help it. It was just how he felt, damn it.

Rogan's smile was sympathetic. "No, you wouldn't, Miller. You'd have gone somewhere else, and you know it. You wanted to run from the bad memories, but you can't. It's all in here—" he tapped the folder with his finger "—all about how your partner—your *female* partner—was killed in the line of duty. She died in your arms at the scene."

Steve made fists of his hands and pressed them against his knees—hard. "And it didn't have to happen. She made a mistake. We stumbled on a big drug deal. I told her to wait for backup, but she went in, anyway."

He shook his head and stared past Rogan and through the window as the anguish of that fateful night washed over him in giant waves. "It didn't have to happen. It shouldn't have happened. Julie took a reckless chance."

"Don't you think you were taking a chance, too, Miller? Getting personally involved with your partner?"

Steve blinked. Surely, that wasn't in his file...

"No, it's not in writing," Rogan said, guessing what he was thinking. "But law enforcement grapevines spread a long way, and rumor has it you and Julie Comstock were having an affair."

Steve couldn't help chuckling over the word. "We were both single. I hardly think it could be considered an affair."

Rogan shrugged. "Whatever. But you did break the rules."

"Rules that are not in writing."

"But it was understood. There's nothing in the manual that says men and women cops can't fraternize, but it's understood they aren't supposed to."

"Well, you won't have to worry about anything happening between me and Liz Casey."

"Good. But you'd better get something straight, here and now. You've got an impressive record, and we're glad to put you to work, but you've got to be a team player, and that means working and getting along with anybody you're assigned.

"And I'm warning you—" he pointed a finger "—don't make waves. The last thing this department needs is a sexual harassment suit. So you treat Casey like an equal, understand?"

Steve bolted to his feet. He was afraid if he didn't leave fast, he might say something he would later regret. "Understood. Anything else?"

Rogan softened. "Yeah." He also rose, holding out his hand. "I want to say welcome aboard...and that I'm real sorry for what happened back in California and hope you'll be happy here."

Steve shook his hand and walked out.

It wasn't quite seven o'clock. He had some time to spare and left the station for coffee and a bagel at the diner across the street.

He had come in early to have the powwow with Rogan and wished now he hadn't, because not only had it been a waste of time, but Rogan would probably let it slip about his protest over a female partner. All eyes would be watching, and he would have to be on his toes to carry out his plan, which was to prove Liz Casey incompetent. Then she would be reassigned to a more suitable position, and he would ultimately be given a male partner.

Sure, he felt some guilt over what he was planning to do, because she was obviously a good cop or she wouldn't have been promoted. But there were many differences between working traffic and being a detective, and, in his opinion, she should not have been moved up the ladder so fast, anyway.

Yeah, there were differences, all right. He had realized that cold, harsh fact when Julie got killed. She had been terrific in patrol, had won a lot of citations, but he felt it had worked against her, making her overly confident. The night she died, she had been reckless—all because she was angry with him.

After it happened, Steve had taken leave to try and deal with his grief...and his guilt. With no family, no responsibilities, he had plenty of time to think, and one day it dawned that he needed to start a new life somewhere else, away from the painful memories.

He picked Alabama because when he was a child, his parents once took him to visit an aunt who lived in Birmingham. He liked the area, and it seemed as good a place as any.

Having made up his mind, he had no trouble getting hired by the Birmingham Police Department.

And here he was, he thought dismally as he pushed the door of the diner open—starting over with the last thing on earth he wanted—a female partner, and an overzealous one who would ticket a fellow cop, to boot.

"Detective Miller, wait, please."

He paused at the sound of a woman's soft voice and drew a ragged breath before turning around, praying it wasn't her.

But it was.

"Detective Miller," Liz Casey repeated as she reached his side. "I'm glad I caught you."

She wasn't short, he noted. Tall, in fact. He hadn't noticed before when he was sitting down in his car. And when she'd been introduced the night before as his new partner, the only thing he saw was red.

She was cute, too, he couldn't help but notice. Coal black hair, big brown eyes, and a turned-up nose with a tiny splash of freckles on the tip.

His eyes flicked over her in a practiced glance, meant to sweep a suspect and take in every detail. She was well built, body toned and tight, no doubt from working out in the police gym. Nicely shaped breasts, accented by a narrow waist, and her high, round buttocks looked good in the tight skirt she was wearing.

She had draped the jacket of her suit casually over her shoulder holster, which held a 9 mm automatic.

"What did you want, Detective Casey?"

"For starters," she said pleasantly, "that we stop being so formal with each other. After all, if we're going to be partners..."

"Yeah, right." He remembered Rogan's warning to tread lightly. Liz Casey, Steve figured, was probably the type to welcome a sexual harassment suit just for the publicity. "How about I call you Casey, and you call me Miller?"

She wrinkled her nose. "Still formal, but if that's what you want—"

"What I want," he said abruptly, so she wouldn't get the idea things between them would ever be warm and fuzzy, "is a cup of coffee. Now is that all you wanted—to get straight about what we're going to call each other?"

He smirked, as though indulging a bothersome child.

Liz stiffened, and the cheerful look on her face quickly disappeared. "Actually, I wanted to apologize about yesterday."

He felt a rush of hope. He didn't want a ticket on his record, for Pete's sake. The guys would razz him to death if they found out, especially over her giving it to him. "Well, that's nice of you, Casey. We all make mistakes. I shouldn't have been speeding even if it was just a few miles over the limit."

"No, you shouldn't, but I didn't have to be so abrupt. It was just a bad day for me, I'm afraid. Too many accidents...the rain and all. And I was soaked, in case you didn't notice." She laughed softly. "Actually it all reminded me of why I worked so hard to get promoted out of traffic to patrol."

"You worked in patrol?"

"Yes, before I was promoted to detective."

"Then why were you working traffic?"

"Doing a friend a favor. Say—" her eyes narrowed "—you didn't think I'd move straight from traffic to detective, did you?"

He didn't answer.

"That's exactly what you thought, wasn't it?" she said, bristling. "That I got pushed to detective because I'm a woman. Well, let me set the record straight, Miller. I've had my training, and if you think otherwise...if that's why you don't want me for a partner, you can stand easy, because I've walked the walk, and I can talk the talk. You haven't got a damn thing to worry about."

Steve knew if his plan to prove her incompetent was to work, they had to stop sparring at every turn. It couldn't look intentional. "Look," he offered. "How about if we start over? I'm sorry if I had the wrong impression about you, okay? I know you wouldn't have made detective grade if you weren't qualified, and I'm sure we'll work out fine together. After all," he added with a quick smile, "if you're willing to apologize and tear up that ticket, the least I can do is admit I've been acting like a jerk."

He motioned her into the diner and followed after her, saying, "I'll even buy you a cup of coffee. How's that?"

"But...but you don't understand," Liz stammered, making no move to go in the direction of the empty booth he was pointing to.

He kept grinning, aware that Mulvaney and some of the detectives also in the diner were watching, waiting to see how he was handling having a female partner. "What's to understand? You were in a bad mood. Maybe I was, too. Let's chalk it up to the weather and forget about it. I'll even buy you breakfast instead of just coffee.''

''No, we can't forget it, because—''

''Because why?'' It was a small diner, and suddenly they had become the center of attention.

She tried again. ''Because—''

''Hey, Miller,'' Mulvaney yelled from where he was sitting at the end of the counter. ''You should've tried to bribe her yesterday—before she gave you the ticket.''

At that, everyone burst into laughter.

Steve, feeling as though he'd been kicked in the gut, looked at Liz. ''How does he know about that?'' he whispered.

''That's what I've been trying to tell you,'' she whispered back. ''I didn't tear up the ticket. I turned it in at Second Precinct, but it was probably posted on the bulletin board at our precinct. They do that when an officer gets a ticket…to embarrass them. I'm sorry.''

Steve was seeing little red dots of anger floating before his eyes. ''But you apologized for yesterday. I thought that meant you tore up the ticket.''

''I apologized because I felt I had handled the situation badly. I never said anything about tearing up the ticket. I'd never do that.''

''No,'' he said quietly, grimly. ''I guess you wouldn't.''

He turned toward the counter, wishing he could just walk out, but knowing it would only make things worse. He had to face the teasing, the razzing, no matter how hard it was.

''Are we okay?'' Liz dared ask.

''Sure,'' he replied, forcing a grin so wide it felt like his face would split, ''but you can buy your own breakfast.''

3

"I'll drive," Steve said.

"Fine," Liz conceded. Steve Miller, she had decided, was the father of all male chauvinists and would probably sooner die than ride in a car with a woman at the wheel.

They were walking across the precinct parking lot, and he was a few paces ahead. Liz did not try to keep up with him, because it seemed to her from the way he was walking that he wanted to distance himself from her as much as possible.

Again, she cursed herself for getting off on the wrong foot with him and wished now that she *had* torn up the ticket.

Actually she wished she hadn't even turned around and gone after him. Five miles over the limit was not so terrible, and, given the fact he was a fellow officer, she would probably have let him off, anyway, had she not been in such a foul mood.

Still, it wasn't fair for him to be mad with her because the other detectives had found out about it, since it hadn't been her fault. Policy dictated that when an officer received a citation of any kind, even in another precinct, it was posted on the bulletin board where he worked. It was meant to embarrass and, in Steve's case, had succeeded.

They reached the car. Steve unlocked her door but did

not offer to open it for her, which was fine. Liz preferred no special consideration because of her gender.

As he was going around to the other side, someone yelled out, "Hey, what's your arresting officer doing, Miller? Giving you driving lessons?"

"Naw," someone else joined in. "It's part of his sentence. Casey's gonna be his probation officer and make sure he goes easy on the pedal."

This was followed by a burst of laughter, and Liz turned to see the same group of detectives that had been in the diner earlier. "Knock it off, guys," she said with a glare. "Next time maybe it'll be one of you caught slamming the pedal to the metal."

They kept on laughing.

"Sorry about that," Liz said as she fastened her seatbelt. "But they'll get tired of it sooner or later, if you make them think they aren't getting to you."

"They aren't," he said curtly. "So drop it."

"Have it your way," she snapped right back. "I was just trying to make you feel better." *What a grouch,* she thought, wondering what she had got herself into. Maybe she should have requested to stay in patrol until she could be assigned a different partner. She could have talked to the chief and explained how there were just bad vibes between her and Miller, and—

"Okay," he said abruptly.

She looked at him. He was gripping the steering wheel and staring at her intently but had made no move to start the car.

She shook her head. "What...?"

"About what happened..."

She tensed in anticipation of another confrontation. How long was he going to carry a grudge? They had to work together, for heaven's sake. Maybe she should declare then and there that it was not going to work, go back inside and ask for her old job back in patrol and just forget about being a detective. She had worked for it, earned it, but if she had to be with the chauvinist-from-hell it wasn't worth it.

"Let's get over it."

Liz wasn't sure she'd heard right. "Did you say what I think you did—that you're willing to forget it?"

"That's right."

"And you aren't mad anymore?"

"If I am, it won't show, okay? After all, it was just a speeding ticket. Small stuff. Thirty-buck fine. It's not worth worrying about."

"I agree."

He flashed a smile. "No hard feelings?"

"I never had any," she said simply. "I was just doing my job."

"With an attitude," he said, smile frozen.

"You gave it to me," she pointed out, "when you tried to talk your way out by flashing your badge."

He started to say something else, then drew a deep breath and let it out in a whoosh. "This isn't getting us anywhere, and it seems like every time we try to have a conversation we wind up fighting."

"I'm not fighting. But you can't blame me for getting huffy when you say I have an attitude."

He threw up his hands, then turned the ignition key. "Why do I bother? We'll never get along."

"Not with *your* attitude," she said haughtily, and folded her arms across her chest.

They rode in silence, and Liz decided the atmosphere could not have been colder had they been riding in a refrigerated truck. Finally she could stand it no longer. "You know, I really don't think this is going to work out. So how about if we go to the chief and tell him there's no point in trying? I mean, partners have to get along. We have to look out for each other, and—''

Steve calmly interrupted to make clear, ''I'll do my part there, Casey, if you'll do yours.''

''Why, sure…''

''Then there's nothing to worry about.'' He held out his hand.

She shook it reluctantly.

''So there's no need to go to the chief,'' he said. ''We'll work things out between us.''

Liz settled back. He sounded sincere. Maybe things *could* work if they set their minds to it. ''I hope so.'' She voiced her thoughts out loud. ''This is something I've wanted for a long, long time.''

Steve wove carefully in and out of the rush hour traffic. There was no need to hurry. Their first assignment was to investigate an armed robbery in a pawnshop. It had happened before dawn. Cops had already scoped out the area but couldn't find the suspect. ''So what made you want to be a cop in the first place?'' he found himself asking her, despite having promised himself not to give a damn about her personally. They would work together—period. And he didn't give a damn what made her tick. Still, there had to be civility, for Pete's sake.

''I'm a third-generation cop,'' she answered proudly. ''My father and grandfather were both officers. Grandpa is dead, but Pop is still on the force down in Montgomery.''

''So how did you wind up in Birmingham?'' he asked, telling himself he didn't really care but reasoning that conversation might ease some of the tension between them. Besides, it would be easier to get rid of her if she didn't think he was hostile toward her.

''I didn't want to live in Dad's shadow,'' she confided.

"He's still on the force in Montgomery, and I didn't want to be known as Sergeant Bill Casey's little girl."

"Any brothers or sisters following in his footsteps, too?"

"Oh, no. I've got two sisters, but they never wanted any part of police work. They both married young."

"And since your father had no sons to carry on the family tradition, you had no choice."

"No. It was what I wanted," she said uneasily, remembering his sarcastic reference to women cops.

"Well, that's good." He turned up the radio. "Be glad you aren't subbing for your friend today," he said as they began to hear wreck reports. "Sounds like it's going to be busy."

"Oh, there's always lots of fender benders during rush hour." She settled back, feeling much better since things seemed to be smoothing out between them.

She looked at him out of the corner of her eye and thought again how attractive he was. And when he smiled, which, so far, had not been often, he had a nice dimple in his cheek that she found adorable.

Her eyes went to his hands on the steering wheel—his *left* hand—and noted he was not wearing a wedding band. "How about you? Are you married?" she asked hesitantly, unsure how he would react to personal questions. But it was only fair after his brief interrogation into her background.

"No," he said curtly. "And I don't plan to be, either."

"That sounds kind of cold, don't you think?"

"Not really. I'm married to my job." He threw her a sharp glance. "In case you haven't realized it, yet, Casey, being a detective isn't a nine-to-fiver."

"Neither was being on patrol, but I didn't mind," she said stiffly.

"But investigations can sometimes be around the clock

for days. I remember working a case in California when I went three nights without sleep. We had a break and wanted to stay on it.

"But," he continued, "it's different for a man. I can't imagine a husband being understanding over the long haul when his wife doesn't come home, especially if there are kids."

"It can be worked out." Liz said uneasily. They had started getting along, and she didn't want to rock the boat. Still, it was hard not to respond to his obviously chauvinistic attitude. "But in case you haven't noticed," she couldn't resist pointing out, "women these days work in all kinds of jobs that were formerly considered only for men."

"Well, you obviously have an understanding husband. That's nice."

"Oh, I'm not married."

They had reached the pawn shop, and he turned into the parking lot without comment.

Liz found herself wondering if she were his first female partner. If not, the ones before her, back in L.A., had probably given up on police work, were in therapy, or selling cookies at a mall somewhere.

She decided to come right out and ask him. "So, is this the first time you've worked with a woman?"

His look was sharp, and there was no mistaking the shadow that crossed his eyes. "What makes you ask that?"

"Just curious. After what you said when I gave you the ticket—about female cops—and the way you've been talking just now, I get the idea you don't like working with women."

"Well, you're wrong. I'm just a private person, Casey, and my job always comes first. You do yours, and we won't have any problems."

It sounded like an ultimatum to Liz, but she bit back a huffy response. He would find out soon enough just how well she could do her job, by damn.

"Hey, I know it's rough moving up to detective," he said as he got out of the car. "I remember when I first started, and I'll help you all I can. Maybe it's good you are single. You don't have to worry about a husband walking the floor wondering if you're okay."

"Been there, done that," she said flippantly.

He slowed his pace so they could walk together. "So you've been married? What happened?"

She saw no reason to lie. "He didn't like being married to a cop. He was—" she couldn't resist the pointed barb "—the sort of sexist who wanted a Barbie doll for a wife, with no ambition beyond Junior League and decorating his arm at cocktail parties."

Steve threw back his head and laughed, then later wanted to kick himself for impulsively quipping, "Well, I can't blame him, Casey. You'd look good on an arm at a cocktail party."

She smiled at the offhanded compliment and began to feel a bit better about things. Maybe Steve Miller had a sense of humor, after all.

Inside the pawnshop, things were chaotic as four policemen tried to calm the very distraught shop owner and his wife.

Officer Bert Winslow, who appeared to be in charge, recognized Liz but had not met Steve and introduced himself.

Steve told him his name, then got down to business. "So what have we got here?"

Liz took out pad and pencil and began to make notes, glad to let Steve ask the questions on her first case. Later she would expect to take turns and let him do the note taking and hoped it would not be a problem.

Winslow recited from his own writing pad what he had learned thus far. "This is Mr. and Mrs. Albertino. They own the place and live upstairs. They were awakened at approximately two-thirty this morning by a masked gunman who made them come down here. He held a gun to Mr. Albertino's head while he opened the safe."

"How much money was in it?" Steve asked as he glanced about the cluttered store.

"No money. Just the expensive stuff—Rolex watches, gold chains, diamonds."

"Any estimate on what the take was worth?"

"Mr. Albertino figures around fifty grand."

Steve checked his watch. "You say the robber woke them up around two-thirty. It's nearly nine now. How long have you been here?"

"Almost two hours. The call was logged in just after seven. No need to look for fingerprints by the way. They said he wore gloves. And they don't want to look at mug shots...said it'd be a waste of time, 'cause he was wearing a mask. They just want us to hurry up and clear out of here so they can call their insurance agent and make a claim and try to get back to normal."

"I still want the fingerprint boys to do their thing. You never know." Steve turned his gaze on the Albertinos. They were sitting side by side in metal folding chairs, arms about each other as they sobbed brokenly.

"Well, I guess you don't need us anymore," Winslow said, sounding eager to abandon the crying couple.

Steve surprised everyone by saying, "I want you guys to hang around awhile."

The officers exchanged glances, and Winslow said, "But

normally when you guys take over, there's nothing else for us to do.''

''Just hang out, okay?'' Steve turned his attention to the Albertinos.

After about fifteen minutes of listening to Steve ask questions that, to Liz, seemed more like what an insurance adjuster would require, she not only thought he was wasting time but also felt left out.

''Excuse me,'' she interrupted, ''but why don't we go ahead and take them in and show them the mug books and see if they can identify the robber?''

The old man exchanged a worried glance with his wife, then said, ''We already told you—he was wearing a mask. We would never be able to identify him.''

Liz pointed out, ''But sometimes there are recognizable features—hair, the shape of the face…''

''No,'' Mr. Albertino said firmly. ''It would be a waste of time.''

His wife's voice caught on a sob. ''I do not want to look at pictures. I want this over with, and I want you people out of here.''

''My wife has been through enough. We both have.''

''Well, I know you're upset,'' Liz argued, ''but if you will just cooperate with us—''

Steve, focused on the couple, murmured to Liz, ''How about letting me handle this, Casey?''

Liz bit back a gasp at his audacity. Why, he had as good as chastised her in front of witnesses…not to mention fellow officers.

She glanced at them out of the corner of her eye. They were stone-faced, not even close to smiling, so they had the decency to ignore her humiliation.

Anger nettled like briars in a blackberry patch as Liz clamped her teeth together to keep from lambasting the arrogant Steve Miller. If he thought he was going to shove her into the background every time they went out on a case, he had another thought coming.

The minutes crawled by as Steve studied the inventory appraisal sheet he had requested from the Albertinos. Finally, he looked Mr. Albertino straight in the eye and said, "Why did you only recently take out insurance on these items, sir?"

The man's eyes went wide. "What do you mean? I have always insured the valuables in my store."

"But for the full value? I mean, it appears you were more concerned over being robbed than you were at not being able to sell your stock and get rid of it so you wouldn't have such a big insurance premium."

Mr. Albertino took out his handkerchief and dabbed at his eyes, then his forehead, which was fast beading with perspiration. "Business has not been good lately," he said, irritated. "Now why do you waste time with foolish questions? You should be trying to catch the person who did this."

Steve smiled. "Oh, believe me, Mr. Albertino, I am trying."

Liz cut her eyes at Steve and wondered whether he might actually be suspecting that the Albertinos knew more than they were letting on. Thinking if they got them to the station it might make them nervous enough to let something slip, she persisted, "I really think we need to take them downtown and show them some mug shots."

"And I told you we don't want to look at your pictures," Mrs. Albertino shrieked, then burst into fresh tears and covered her face with her hands.

"Why not?" Steve calmly asked her. "Why aren't you willing to try to identify the man who robbed you?"

Liz chimed in, wanting to be a party to cracking the case

if Steve was on the right track. "I really think it would help, Mrs. Albertino. So come with us to the station, and—"

Inclining his head ever so slightly, Steve whispered, "Casey, please." Then, to the woman, asked, "How many children do you have, Mrs. Albertino?"

She raised her head to stare at him sharply. "Why do you ask that? What difference does it make?"

Mr. Albertino put his arm around his wife and angrily said to Steve, "Detective, you have wasted enough of our time with your foolish questions."

"You have a son, don't you?"

Mrs. Albertino, turning pale, shook her head and stammered, "No...yes...I...what difference does it make? He is not here."

"No," Steve said quietly, "I wouldn't expect him to be. I imagine he's real busy this morning trying to find a fence for all the stuff he took from the safe."

"What—" Mr. Albertino started to rise from his chair, but Steve motioned him to stay where he was.

Liz had turned away to lean against a counter in exasperation, but whipped around.

The other officers, stunned, moved in closer.

Steve proceeded slowly, gently. "You set this up with your son, didn't you? He's probably in some kind of trouble and needed the money, but it will go easier if you get it all out in the open now without making me dig for it."

Mr. and Mrs. Albertino comforted each other as they cried.

Steve leaned back and waited.

It did not take long.

Mr. Albertino calmed first, and, with shoulders slumped in defeat, confirmed everything. His son, he said, was deep in debt from his drug habit. Dealers he owed had threatened his life if he didn't pay up. "He said if we would help him, he would give up the drugs, but if we didn't, he was a dead man."

Steve drew a long, shuddering breath and let it out as a ragged sigh, then motioned to the officers. "I think these people are about to give us the name and description of the robber. As soon as they do, get out an APB, then book them as accessories before the fact."

Liz could only stand and stare in wonder...all the while wishing she had asserted herself by asking questions of her own, rather than just continuing to insist the Albertinos view mug shots.

She also knew by the way the officers were looking at her that they thought so, too.

Steve Miller had bested her.

He had been instantly suspicious about the Albertinos' eagerness to file an insurance claim and put the robbery behind them, as well as their refusal to even try to identify the culprit.

He had seized on it, seen it through, and in no time flat had solved the case.

And, as if she hadn't been feeling bad enough already, Steve thumped on her coffin lid by brightly saying, loud enough for the other cops to hear, of course, "Hey, don't feel bad, Casey. I played a hunch and won. It's called experience. And if you stick it out long enough, one day you might have it."

There were a few chuckles, and Casey felt her blood boil like water rolling in a kettle.

"Oh, don't worry," she managed to say without gritting her teeth or clenching her fists, "I plan to stick like Super-glue, Miller."

4

Steve was the talk of the precinct.

The following morning at roll call, the chief himself showed up to praise Steve for his intuition. Realizing that the pawnshop robbery had been set up between the parents and their drug addict son had been quite a coup.

If only all detectives, the chief raved on, could have the same kind of insight, the money and manpower hours saved would be phenomenal.

"That couple could have tied up the department for days on end looking through every mug shot book we've got," the chief pointed out.

At that, Steve, standing beside him in the front of the room, stole a glance at Liz. The chief wasn't aware of how she had insisted that the Albertinos do just that, and probably no one else noticed that she looked as if she wanted to crawl in a hole and pull it in after her.

But Steve told himself it was what he wanted—for her to feel inept and ultimately quit. If she wanted to remain in police work, let her do so in a safer department.

Still, he couldn't help feeling badly about what he had to do. She was, after all, sincere in her desire to do a good job.

And he couldn't help noticing, she was also beautiful.

He liked her face and the mischievous tilt of her nose.

And even at their first encounter, when he'd been mad to busting, he hadn't been able to help noticing her full, pouty lips and thinking how it might feel to kiss her.

He had also taken note, when she'd turned from his car after writing him up, that she had a nice shape. She had been wearing the requisite blue trousers with a darker blue stripe down the sides, and, being wet, they molded her tight bottom even tighter.

The same was true of her shirt, and he had enjoyed the eye-level view despite his rage.

Steve chided himself big-time whenever he allowed such thoughts to creep over him. He had to stay focused on making her want to quit without it seeming he had anything to do with it. It wasn't only for her good, but his own, as well, so the last thing he needed was to feel attraction for her, damn it.

The chief was winding up his speech, and Steve was glad. The other detectives were beginning to fidget in their seats, and it was time to get on with something else. Otherwise they were going to resent him and think of him as being a show-off hotshot from the infamous LAPD, and he damn well didn't want that, either.

Steve swallowed a smile, however, when the chief concluded by pointing straight at Liz and saying, "You're fortunate to have a partner like Miller, Casey. You can learn a lot."

Her smile, Steve knew, was obligatory. It also lasted only a fraction of a second before she seemed to turn into an ice sculpture.

The chief shook Steve's hand again. "There'll be a letter of commendation in your file, Miller. Keep up the good work. We're proud to have you on the force."

Grateful it was over, Steve left the podium and slid into the vacant seat next to Liz.

She did not acknowledge his presence.

The chief left. Roll call continued, followed by progress reports of investigations under way and new assignments doled out.

"Nothing for you two," Walt Rogan said with a nod to Steve and Liz at the end of the meeting. "But don't worry. You're next in line for anything that comes in, and before long you'll have a backlog of cases like everybody else. Why don't you take advantage of the free time at the firing range?"

"Sounds like a good idea to me," Steve said as he and Liz joined the others filing out of the room. Having won department sharpshooter honors for three years straight back in L.A., he figured it might be another way to show her up and make her feel less than qualified.

She shrugged. "Why not? It's either that or hang around waiting for the phone to ring."

"Hey, don't knock it," Mulvaney, walking behind them, warned. "You two are lucky. This is the first easy spell we've had in quite a while. But I guess you deserve a reward for being so smart yesterday, huh, Miller?"

"I was just doing my job," Steve said soberly.

"And a good one, too. And maybe," Mulvaney added with a sly grin as he slapped him on the shoulder, "it even makes up for the speeding rap, huh?"

Steve retorted, "Yeah, maybe it does, Mulvaney. And maybe one of these days she'll be around when you're off duty and your foot gets heavy."

Liz couldn't resist pointing out, "Don't worry, Mulvaney. I don't do traffic anymore. I was just filling in for somebody." Then, hoping to make Brownie points with Steve, gave him a playful poke and impishly said, "Is he really a speed demon, Miller? I can tell my friend to keep an eye out."

The grin disappeared from Mulvaney's face like sunshine on a cloudy day. "You don't need to worry about me, but hey, Casey—" he snapped his fingers "—I just thought of something. I heard how you're really big on wanting victims to look at mug shots. So why don't you take advantage of all this free time to go through the books and straighten them up? Last I heard, they were a real mess. You can do that and leave the hard stuff to Miller."

Steve saw anger flashing in Liz's eyes and knew she was biting back her temper. He did feel sorry for her, but what was happening was for her own good, and he seized the chance to appear to be defending her while actually setting her up for even more humiliation when it got out how he had bested her on the firing range. "Cool it, Mulvaney." He made his tone gruff. "We're going to the shooting range."

They walked on out, and once they were alone, Liz lashed out at him. "Wasn't it enough you showed me up in front of those cops you purposely asked to hang around because you were hoping you'd be able to? Did you have to blab it all over the precinct so Mulvaney, the big jerk, would hear about it?

"Besides," she raged on, "it was only natural I'd ask the victims to look at pictures. Why make such a big deal out of it because you had a hunch and it paid off?"

Lips curving in a lazy smile, he insolently asked, "Feel better now that you've let me have it?"

"Let you have it?" she echoed, bewildered. "What are you talking about? I only asked why you have to try and make me look even more foolish than I already feel."

Steve heard a warning bell and immediately moved to quash her suspicion. "Hey, wait a minute. I never said a word, and I'm sorry those cops in the pawnshop did, because they have to be the ones responsible for it getting out. I swear to you I never said anything.

"And as for me asking them to hang around," he said to further get himself off the hook, "I only did that in case they'd be able to offer something that might tell us where the suspect might have gone. You know…like a mannerism he might have had that made them think of somebody in the neighborhood.

"The cops," he finished, "were there to do the leg work if it was necessary, so you and I wouldn't have to."

They were standing in the hall outside the indoor shooting range.

Liz looked at him long and hard.

Steve knew she was wondering whether he was telling the truth when finally, with a sigh, she said, "Okay. So I'm wrong. I guess I'm just looking for someone to blame for my own stupidity."

"It wasn't stupidity, because you're right—it was the logical thing to do to ask them to look at mug shots. But I dialed in right away to how they were so adamantly against it, as well as how they wanted us out of there so they could call their insurance adjuster and get the ball rolling on filing a claim."

Liz said, "Well, one day maybe I'll have that same kind of intuition. For now I guess it's like the chief said—I can learn a lot from you."

"As for Mulvaney and those clowns, you know you can always go to the chief and claim sexual harassment."

"But I don't think my being a woman has anything to do with it. They'd tease me if I were a man."

"Are you sure about that?" He would love for her to accuse somebody else of what he was surreptitiously doing himself. It would make things a lot easier…and quicker.

She gave her head a determined shake. "Nope. I disagree

with you. They haven't made one remark that gives me cause to think the motive is sexism. Besides, they really don't mean any harm. I've just got to have thicker skin. I can't go around getting all bent out of shape over good-natured teasing like you did over that silly speeding ticket.

"And I hope to goodness you're over that by now," she finished, eyes twinkling once more.

She was standing so close he could smell the sweet scent of soap and bath powder...could see the golden lights dancing in her soft eyes.

"Sure I have," he said, then decided a little flattery wouldn't hurt. After all, he did find her attractive, and what was the harm in being nice along the way to getting rid of her?

He smiled. "But I wonder what you consider a sexist remark? For instance, what if I say I like the way you wear your hair, or that I think you've got a nice figure, and I like that little freckle on the tip of your nose? Can't a guy compliment a lady without being sexist...or being guilty of harassment?"

"Uh, I suppose so," she stammered.

"Good, because I just did," he grinned, "and if I'm a sexist, or if I'm harassing, so be it."

He opened the door to the firing range and stood back for her to enter first, all the while aware of the puzzled way she was looking at him.

The officer in charge of the range issued their ammunition.

They took windows side by side.

"You like shooting, do you?" Steve asked Liz as he slipped the loaded clip into his gun.

"Yeah," she replied with cool confidence. Her clip already loaded, she adjusted the sound-cushioning muffs on her ears. "My dad had me shooting as soon as my hand was big enough to hold a pistol. Made Mom furious, too. She hates guns."

Steve watched as she pulled the string to adjust the target and saw that she was placing it as far away as it would go. "What are you doing that for? We always concentrate on close encounters."

"It doesn't hurt to be accurate at every distance."

He was pleased to see that just then the door opened and Mulvaney and a couple of his cohorts walked in to watch. Good. That meant they would see him outshoot her, which would increase her feelings of inadequacy.

"Well, go ahead, Calamity Jane," he said with a chuckle, "but you're just wasting ammo..."

He was drowned out by the deafening sound as Liz rapidly fired off six rounds.

Steve didn't acknowledge the presence of the other officers. Neither did he pay any attention to Liz as he proceeded to set up his own targets. He knew when it was all over, he would be the sharpshooter and Liz, if anything, would prove only good enough to meet the force's requirements.

But as it turned out, Steve was the one with a red face.

"Hey, would you look at that?" Mulvaney cried. He was standing behind Liz as she drew all of her targets forward. He gave a long, low whistle. "Wow, she hit the bull's-eye dead center with every shot at every distance. Nobody in the department has ever done that, that I know of.

"Even you, Miller." He turned to Steve with a big smirk on his face.

At first Steve thought he was lying, trying to be cute. Stepping into Liz's cubicle, he checked the targets himself and hoped he was successful in keeping his eyes from bugging out to see the results.

As Mulvaney had said, she had a perfect score.

There was applause and cheers. Word spread quickly, and everyone in the precinct seemed to find their way to the range to congratulate Liz. No one had been aware she was such a good shot. She had always practiced when the range was empty. Afraid everyone would think she was showing off, it had been her little secret—till now.

"It's nothing, really," she said humbly. "Like I told Steve, my dad had a gun in my hand when most kids are still holding rattles."

"But a perfect score?" someone marveled.

She shrugged, as though it were nothing. "Just lucky."

Walt Rogan had shown up, and he put a hand on Steve's shoulder as he said, "If you had checked your partner's record, you'd have found out she's classified as a sharpshooter."

"I had no reason to check her record," Steve said tightly. "And we weren't having a match, for crying out loud."

Suddenly he realized he sounded like a child, and from the looks some of the other officers were giving him knew they thought so, too.

"Well, you weren't so bad yourself, Miller," Mulvaney said as he looked over Steve's targets. "Just a little bit off. I'd say you two would be considered the sharpest shooters in the precinct."

Larry Spicer, Mulvaney's partner, guffawed and said, "Maybe they should be split up to share the accuracy. I'd damn sure rather have a shooter like Casey for a partner than somebody like you who has a problem hitting anywhere on the sheet."

Everyone laughed, including Casey, who was, Steve suspected, enjoying the camaraderie and sense of belonging much more than the praise.

Things, he decided, were not going at all as he had expected. And, with his latest scheme backfiring, the fact that he had shown her up at the pawnshop was forgotten. So he was going to have to work all the harder.

The crowd broke up. People went back to whatever they had been doing when they'd heard about a perfect score in the shooting range.

Feigning cheeriness, Steve said, "Well, I guess there's no need in hanging around here. We've both proved we can handle a gun."

"That's for sure. You're good, too, Steve."

He bristled, thinking she was patronizing him, then told himself not to let the situation turn him into a real grump.

They picked up their spent shells, cleaning up around the cubicles as required, then turned everything in at the desk.

On the way out, Steve said he was going to take the car they had been assigned for a spin to make sure everything was okay. "I noticed a funny sound in the engine, and it has to be in top shape at all times. Just beep me if you need me."

He thought she looked disappointed and wondered if she was...if she wanted to be with him...then reminded himself it didn't matter if she did.

"Well, okay," she said finally. "I'm going to study the unsolved crimes file."

Steve knew that was what detectives usually did in idle moments—of which there were precious few—and what he would have done under ordinary circumstances. But circumstances were no longer ordinary for him—not since Liz Casey had walked into his life with all the subtlety of a bear crashing a picnic. And the fact was he needed some time alone, because being around her was provoking thoughts that had nothing to do with getting rid of her.

"You do that," he said, turning in the opposite direction.

He had gone only a few steps when she called, "Steve, wait a minute."

She hurried to catch up with him, searching his face with anxious eyes. "You aren't mad about my getting a perfect score, are you? I mean, I wasn't trying to show off or anything. I just happen to be a good shot."

He told himself to ignore how her blouse stretched tightly across her breasts as she waved her arms as she talked, a habit, he had noted, when she felt passionate about whatever she was saying.

He wasn't supposed to notice anything about her physical appearance. Hell, he wasn't even supposed to notice she was a woman—just his partner—but he would have to be blind not to.

He laughed. "What? Are you crazy? That didn't bother me at all. Besides, I leave the paranoia to you, Casey."

"What do you mean?"

"Like you thinking I asked those cops to hang back at the pawnshop to show you up. That's paranoia." He gave her a playful cuff on the chin, thinking how nice it would be to give her a hug instead. But he didn't dare. It might lead to something else—like kissing her as he found himself yearning to do. "You need to lighten up, kid. You worry too much. Now go check out the files."

He started to walk away, then turned his head to grin and say, "And while you're at it, clean up the mug shot books."

"Oh, you..." She laughed and waved him away.

The mood was light. Everything was okay. Steve felt better and would simply retreat to rethink his strategy.

He would, by golly, find a way to prove that she just wasn't cut out for the job.

And then he could get on with his job, and his life, and keep the vow he had made to himself to never, ever again get involved with a woman who was in his line of work.

5

—◆—

"So how's the poor man's Dirty Harry?" Carol Batson greeted Liz as she breezed into her apartment.

"Dirty Harry, indeed," Liz sneered. "Dumb Dora is more like it. I've been a detective for over two weeks now, and I feel absolutely useless."

Carol saw the just-delivered pizza on the coffee table and smacked her lips in anticipation. "Pepperoni. My favorite. And look—you remembered I hate anchovies. Ah, what a friend."

She flopped down on the sofa and helped herself to a big slice, then talked around it to ask, "So tell me why you're beating yourself over the head with a night stick? What's this Dumb Dora business?"

With a sigh, Liz also settled on the sofa, curling her legs beneath her. "You mean you haven't heard?"

"Heard what?" Carol giggled as she pulled at a long string of melted cheese. "We traffic cops don't get much scuttlebutt from upstairs—especially in another precinct."

"I made a classic goof on my first case." Liz told her what had happened in the pawnshop.

"So?" Carol took a big swallow of Coke. "That doesn't sound like a big deal to me."

"But ever since then we've had little nothing cases.

Steve solved them quicker than one of those find-a-word puzzles.''

"So? If 'The Hunk' is sharp, good for him.''

"'The Hunk'? You mean Steve?''

"We're talking about your partner, aren't we?''

"I was under that impression, yes.''

"And he's a hunk, right?''

"Well...''

Carol laughed. "Oh, come on, Liz. You can level with me. We're old buddies. All the gals are whispering about him. The guy is drop-dead gorgeous. And don't pretend you haven't noticed. Lies don't go with pepperoni, you know.'' She pointed at the pizza. "Hey, you aren't eating.''

"Well, I thought I was hungry, but I'm not.''

Carol shrugged. "More for me. But listen—back to Miller—seriously, he is good-looking, and I don't mind telling you we single gals envy you.''

Liz threw up her hands. "I'd like to know what for. Even if I were attracted to him—which I'm not,'' she emphasized, "it's against regulations for male and female officers to fraternize, and you know it.''

And besides that, Liz thought grimly, the last thing she needed was to get involved with someone she suspected was as opposed to women cops as Craig had been.

Carol was not about to give up. "And when has that stopped anybody? Besides, there's no written regulation. It's just sort of understood. The powers-that-be discourage it, that's all. Don't you remember that couple in patrol who got married last summer? All they did was transfer one of them to another precinct.''

"Carol, forget it.'' Liz shook her head. "Even if I were interested in Steve Miller—which I'm not,'' she repeated, stronger this time, "he would never be interested in me.''

"Why not?''

"He's got this thing about women being on the force."

Carol's eyes bugged. "He told you that? He actually told you he's against it?" She slapped her forehead, leaving a smear of pizza sauce. "Oh, man. He could lose his job, and you could sue the city if he makes things rough for you. Wow. The guy might be good-looking, but he's not very bright when it comes to policy."

Liz hurried to stop that line of thinking before Carol got carried away. She adored her, but she had a habit of exaggerating things. "Wait a minute. You've got it all wrong. He just made a sarcastic remark about women cops when I wrote him up, that's all."

"And he's okay with you for a partner after that?" Carol swung her head from side to side. "I don't think so, girlfriend."

"Well, he says he is." Liz defended him, having decided, after much thought, to give Steve Miller the benefit of the doubt. She would not, by golly, let a snide remark in a stressful moment cause paranoia. As for him asking the cops to hang around at the pawnshop, he had explained that.

"And you're comfortable with him?"

"Yes."

Carol shrugged. "Then okay. So maybe the two of you will cozy up."

"I'm a career cop, remember?" Liz said with a slight edge to her voice. She and Carol had had this conversation many times. Carol was happy working in traffic, because she had no real ambition beyond finding a husband...no goal beyond her present position.

Carol snatched up yet another slice of pizza and shook it at her as she said, "What you're going to do is wind up all alone living on your pension if you don't loosen up.

Here you've got a golden opportunity to snag a real dream guy, and you don't even care.''

"No," Liz curtly confirmed. "And I'm not going to worry about it, and I wish you wouldn't, either."

"Well, I just think it's sad you let one jerk sour you on men."

Liz leaned closer in an unconscious gesture meant for Carol to feel the intensity of her declaration, "I am not sour on men. It just so happens that I haven't found one that I am attracted to. Neither am I actively looking, because I promised myself when Craig and I broke up that I was not going to become one of those desperate females that go out looking for a man to prove to themselves they still have it what it takes to get one."

Carol also leaned in closer. "Nobody says you have to, but neither do you have to close and bolt the door to your heart to prove it, either, and—'' She screamed as a cat suddenly appeared from out of nowhere to leap in her lap, then land right in the middle of the pizza. "Oh, no. Look what he's done. I hate cats."

Liz quickly scooped him up. "How can you hate Tom? He's a sweetie pie. He's just playful and mischievous, that's all."

Carol screwed her face in disgust as she brushed at her T-shirt to get rid of any clinging hairs. "When did you get a cat? Good grief, if I'd known you had one, I wouldn't have come over here."

Liz was undaunted. "Oh, yes, you would. You can't turn down pizza. Besides, I didn't get Tom—he got me. He just showed up at my door one night, walked in, liked what he saw and stayed."

"And you named him Tom? Not very original."

"Maybe so, but he's an original tomcat, so it seemed logical to call him that."

Carol scoffed, "So now you're going to be a spinster with a cat." She gave an exaggerated sigh. "I suppose that's logical, too."

"Now you're being dramatic." Liz wiped off the cat's paws with a napkin, set him on the floor, then took what was left of the pizza into the kitchen and trashed it.

When she got back to the living room, Carol was standing at the front door motioning her to hurry. "Come on. We've still got time to make it."

Liz was baffled. "Make *what?*"

"The free pizza buffet on Friday nights at the Blue Spot Bar. They stop serving at eight o'clock, and then you have to order it and pay for it."

Liz could not help laughing at Carol's insatiable appetite for pizza. And how she could stuff herself at will and never gain an ounce was beyond comprehension. Still, Liz was not wild about the Blue Spot, where the single cops could be found on Friday nights hitting on each other—*against policy,* of course. And she always felt it made her look desperate to go there.

"I don't know, Carol," she hedged.

"Oh, what else have you got to do besides sit here with that stupid cat? It'll do you good. Besides, how often do we both have Friday nights off together? Now get your buns in gear, and let's go."

Liz did not want to but knew Carol would not give up. "All right, but I do so in protest," she said, grabbing up her purse and following her out the door.

The place was packed. Music blared from speakers, making it difficult to carry on a conversation. Beer flowed like water, and, of course, there was plenty of pizza.

"I like it because the crowd changes according to who's on what shift," Carol said with enthusiasm. She was helping herself to as much pizza as her paper plate could hold at one time. "There's always somebody new, 'cause guys come from every precinct in town. How long has it been since you were here?"

Drily, Liz retorted, "Since the last time you dragged me. I can't remember...and don't want to. I feel like I'm a part of the buffet, for gosh sakes."

"What's that supposed to mean?"

Liz leaned to whisper, "Don't you see how those guys lined up at the bar are looking at us?"

Carol grinned, "I sure do, and as soon as I finish eating I'm going to look right back."

"I give up," Liz groaned.

Carol led the way to a table. "Isn't this great?" she gushed. "I mean, we've got a place to hang out that's all our own."

Liz pointed out, "I have a place to hang out that's all my own."

"Yeah," Carol sniffed. "And you share it with a cat."

Leaning back in her chair, Liz wondered how long she would have to stay. Sooner or later one of the guys at the bar would amble over and hit on Carol. Liz knew she could leave then, because Carol would no longer care if she were around or not. Fifteen minutes. A half hour at the most. Then she could escape.

Suddenly Carol gave her a sharp nudge with her elbow. "Do you see who I see?"

Liz glanced around. "No. What..." And then she sucked in her breath. Steve Miller was at the end of the bar talking to Mulvaney. "So?" she managed to say thinly.

"So he doesn't have a date, which is a good sign he's unattached."

"And I should care, right?" Liz scoffed, all the while telling her heart to slow down. Carol was right. Steve Miller was a hunk. And the more time she spent with him, she found other things about him appealing as well, like his keen wit and sense of humor. And then there was the serious, analytical side and how he seemed to be able to look right inside a suspect and tell what he was thinking. Dark, brooding, sensitive and sharp. He was a good cop and a nice guy—but Liz had no intentions of making a fool of herself by letting him know in any way that she was even remotely interested in him as a man. He was her partner and nothing more.

Carol continued her goading. "If you had a brain in your head, you'd care."

"Then I have no brains."

"You can say that again."

Liz felt a twinge of annoyance. "Look, I didn't come here for you to nag at me, so maybe I'll just run along and let you have all the fun."

"Oh, get the starch out of your panty hose, Casey. Lighten up. Why do you have to be so serious all the time? Why can't you just relax and enjoy—oh, my God."

"What?" Liz saw Carol staring beyond her like she had seen Elvis.

"He's coming over here."

"Who?"

"Miller. He's seen us, and he's coming over. Listen—" she grabbed Liz's arm and squeezed "—if you don't want him, can I have him?"

"What?"

"Just kidding," she said with a giggle.

Liz sighed and shook her head, wondering how in the world a clown like Carol had ever made it onto the force.

"Hi, partner," Steve cheerily greeted when he reached the table. He looked at Carol. "I don't believe we've met."

Carol introduced herself, then informed him, "I'm the

traffic cop Liz was filling in for when she wrote you up. I heard you really took a ragging about that.''

Liz kicked her under the table. "Don't pay any attention to her," she said to Steve. "She's got a big mouth. I try to keep it filled with pizza to avoid having to listen to it."

He glanced at Carol's plate and grinned. "Well, it looks like you're doing a good job."

Carol, used to being teased about her passion for pizza, was undaunted. "I'm willing to share. Have a seat."

"Don't mind if I do."

Liz felt like kicking her again—harder.

"That's basically why I come here," he said to no one in particular. "They have great pizza."

"Some people come to meet other people," Carol said coyly. "You know—boys meet girls, stuff like that. You ever meet anybody here?" she suddenly, bluntly, asked.

Liz had decided that if Carol wanted to look like an idiot, so be it. Staring toward the dance floor, she pretended to be totally absorbed in watching one of the detectives doing a mean Texas two-step with a female motorcycle cop, both of them having a wonderful time.

Carol babbled on, and Steve politely responded. Then, after a few moments, Liz couldn't help but glare at her when she said, "So how does it feel to be stuck with the only female detective in first precinct, Miller?"

"Quite frankly, I'm honored," he said.

Liz swallowed a gasp.

"Really?" Carol asked.

"Really. The fact is," he went on to explain, "her being the only—and first—for our precinct can be a rather delicate situation. It can sort of be equated to the first female students at a previously all-male military academy. I'm fortunate that Liz fits right in. She asks for no special privileges. She's just one of the guys."

Carol yelped. "One of the guys? That's how you see her? As cute as she is?"

"Oh, Carol, that does it." Liz started to get up, but Steve gently fastened his hand around her wrist to hold her back.

"She's just having fun," he said, amused. "Like Mulvaney and the other guys every chance they get. Pay no attention."

To Carol he said, "And, yes, she is cute, but that has nothing to do with the fact she's a good detective, and I like working with her. I wouldn't want another partner."

Liz caught herself in time to keep her mouth from gaping open.

Then Steve was turning to her with a somewhat apologetic expression to say, "You know, I'm almost sorry we haven't had some meatier cases. I don't think you worked to make detective to handle the boring stuff that's been thrown our way. But, it's been that way, I suppose, because they want to break us in easy."

Carol interjected, "Yeah, she was just saying earlier how she feels like a Dumb Dora, because you've solved all the cases you've had so far, and—"

"Carol," Liz said with careful control, since she was very near to losing her patience, "I think I saw them put a fresh pepperoni pizza out. Maybe you should get over there before everyone else does, and..." Her voice trailed off to silence as Carol nearly turned her chair over in her haste to get to the buffet table.

"I'm sorry," Liz murmured. "She means no harm. She just talks too much."

"Oh, I know that. She's actually funny. But tell me—" he leaned closer and propped his chin on his hand as he stared at her intently "—what's this 'Dumb Dora' thing?"

"Well," Liz made little circles on the table with her Coke glass. "I just don't feel like I'm carrying my part of the load on this team. Every time we've had a case, it seems you solved it before I even knew what was going on. You didn't need me.''

''You shouldn't feel like that.'' Steve was trying very hard not to let it show how pleased he was that she did. Obviously his scheme was working, and if it continued, it was just a matter of time till she put in for a transfer back to patrol.

It was also bothering him, more than he cared to think about, how he was going to miss her when she did. More and more he looked forward to reporting to work just to be around her.

''But I do feel that way,'' she said.

''Well, if I were in your shoes, maybe I would, too,'' he said carefully, fighting the impulse to reach out and touch her in comfort. ''But the assignments won't stay easy and simple. You'll have your chance.''

Her soft laugh rang hollow. ''I hope so, because I have to say I enjoyed patrol more. Being a detective isn't as exciting as I thought it would be.''

''Maybe you watched too many 'N.Y.P.D. Blue' too often.'' He signaled to a waitress. ''Let me buy you a drink. I saw you sitting over here and thought you looked kind of down.''

''Maybe I shouldn't have whiskey. After all, Friday nights can get pretty wild. If we got a call, I'd hate like heck to have a drink under my belt.''

''But we won't get one. We're off duty, remember? It would take a real emergency to pull us in, so we're safe. Now what'll it be?''

''Frozen Margarita.''

''What about Carol?''

Liz pretended to growl. ''Let her buy her own.''

"Ah, come on." He grinned and told the waitress to bring two Margaritas and one scotch and water.

Carol came back in time to see the waitress walk away. "Hey, I need a drink, too."

"It's been ordered," Steve assured, then noted she only had two slices of pizza on her plate. "What's wrong? You lost your appetite?"

"No. Liz ordered a pizza at her place earlier, and I managed to get a few slices before Tom arrived. He pretty well took care of the rest of it."

"He's your boyfriend? Why didn't you bring him along?"

Liz interrupted to try and explain, "No, Tom is my—"

Carol, eyes impishly shining, rushed to say, "That's right. Tom is her boyfriend, and he didn't come because he wanted to stay home and watch the fights—and chow down the rest of the pizza," she added.

Liz protested, "No, wait—"

But just then a voice came over the loudspeaker, "Steve Miller. You have a call."

Steve gave a little gasp and slapped at his waist. "Damn it. I took my beeper out to put a new battery in and left it home."

Liz was likewise embarrassed. "And I didn't think to bring mine, and we're supposed to wear them even if we are off duty. Oh, gosh, I hope it's not a call for us."

"I've got an idea it is," he said, bolting to his feet. "This is the first place they'd look for me, if they couldn't beep me or reach me by phone."

"Is that true? You hang out here a lot?" Carol asked, but he was already on his way to the phone. She turned to Liz. "Do you think that's true? I would've seen him if he'd been hanging out here much, or one of the other girls would have said something, and—"

"And I think if you say one more word to embarrass me," Liz warned, "you are going to be wearing that damn pizza instead of eating it."

"Now what did I do?"

"As if you didn't know. 'Tom is her boyfriend,'" she mimicked. "Why did you say a dumb thing like that?"

"Well, you don't want him to think you don't date anybody, do you?"

"I don't care what he thinks."

"You should," Carol said haughtily. "And if you're smart, you'll keep on letting him believe Tom is your live-in and not your stupid cat."

Liz made a twisting motion with her hands. "If you only knew how easy it would be to strangle you here and now, Carol Batson, you'd jump and run and keep on going. In fact—" she reached for her bag "—if that call isn't for me and Steve, I'm out of here."

"You're out of here, all right," Steve said, suddenly appearing at her side to catch the last of her words. "But you're going with me." He took out his wallet and threw some money on the table to pay for the drinks they would not be having. "Let's go."

"Where?" Liz was rushing to keep up with him.

"Robbery in progress," he threw over his shoulder as they pushed through the crowd. "All the other teams are out. Seems there's a full moon tonight, and the crazies are on the move."

Liz felt a shiver of excitement. "What's the location?"

"Liquor store," he said grimly. "And it gets worse."

"What do you mean?"

"It's a hostage situation."

Liz groaned. "Correction, Miller— 'It don't get no worse.'"

He could have told her how right she was, for he knew only too well.

It had been the same kind of scenario when Julie had been killed, and, oh, Lord, how he wished he weren't heading into bad memories with another female partner.

6

"I'm not exactly dressed for this, you know," Liz said. She was wearing a button-down cardigan and skirt that were casual...maybe even a little sexy, even though the sweater was loose enough to hide her shoulder holster.

Steve was gripping the steering wheel with both hands, careful and alert as he sped around traffic in his haste to get to the crime scene. "It doesn't matter. Besides—" he shot her a quick glance and smiled "—you look great. You've got nice legs."

Liz felt her cheeks grow warm and stole a glance of her own in his direction. He was wearing a turtleneck that stretched deliciously across his broad, muscular chest. It was an appealing change from the white shirt and tie he usually wore.

"Thanks," she murmured softly, then, attempting to ease the almost electrical tension that had suddenly dropped over them like a shroud, she added, "At least I carry my gun when I'm off duty, so I'm prepared."

"Then let's not worry about it. We need to concentrate on what we're going up against." He reached for the mike. He always kept the unmarked car they had been issued. Though he had offered to take turns, Liz said she preferred he keep it all the time.

"Unit seven to base." He spoke fast and tense.

"What've you got on the yahoo holed up in the liquor store on Tenth and Broad?"

"Male. Caucasian," Carl Bundy came right back. "Cops on the scene called in the license plate of the vehicle believed to belong to the suspect."

Liz could not help smiling to think how ridiculous they always used the term suspect, regardless of the circumstances. The man in the liquor store was not suspected of being the lawbreaker—he *was* the lawbreaker. But there were a lot of strange rules she did not understand that had to be strictly followed.

"Booker, Alan," Bundy continued. "Age twenty. Released on parole two months ago after doing two of five for possession and attempted burglary."

"*Attempted?*" Liz questioned.

Bundy responded, "Yeah. He got caught before he could actually break in, and he had a good lawyer that got the jury to swallow it. Ain't that a scream? Otherwise, he'd still be in Kilby."

Steve asked, "Did he have an accomplice tonight?"

"No sign of one."

"Get hold of his parole officer and have him report to the scene. Ten-four," Steve signed off.

The blue strobe on the top of the car spun eerie light into the darkness.

Liz ran her fingers up and down her arms. It was a tense time, and she was no stranger to such a situation. But in the past she had been in training, observing from a safe distance and not as a participant.

Steve was uptight, too. She could feel it. Still, she was astonished to hear him say, "You know the procedure, right?"

"Well, I should think so," she said with a soft laugh.

"I mean, I did have some training for this job, you know. They didn't exactly find me under a cabbage leaf."

She was stunned by his sudden explosion of anger.

"Don't smart mouth me, Casey. This is serious. I know damn well you've had training." He spoke as fast as a rapid-fire 9mm Glock. "The requisite twenty-five sit-ups, thirty consecutive trigger pulls, and twenty-two push ups. You've scaled a fence six feet high, dragged a 165-pound dummy fifteen feet, walked on a balance beam and shimmied through a two-foot-square window. You've passed all the tests for endurance.

"But none of it means a damn thing," he raged on, lifting one hand from the steering wheel to make a fist and shake it. "Not when you're in a situation like this. You hang back and keep your cool and analyze everything before you act, understand?"

She stared at him in wonder. Never had she seen him so mad or upset. He seemed close to being out of control, which was so out of character for someone always so cool and focused.

"Steve, what is wrong with you?" she asked timorously. "You don't have to lecture me. If I weren't qualified, I wouldn't be here."

"We just went through that, and I acknowledge that you are, but you've got to follow rules here. Don't take any chances, understand? The guy knows his number is up, and he's going back to Kilby to do some hard time. He's desperate, which means he won't bat an eye at killing somebody."

Liz was having a real hard time responding instead of reacting. "What you're trying to say is that you're in charge here, right? Okay, fine."

"Just don't do anything impulsive." He turned into the

parking lot of the liquor store on two wheels, spraying gravel.

Though she was furious, Liz managed to get a grip on herself. They had only been working together two weeks, and there would be time later to let him know she was not going to take that kind of crap whenever they were called to a crisis situation. She did not deserve it, and he had no right to lash out at her, by God.

There was only one patrol car on the scene. She noted how curious onlookers were keeping a safe distance, which was good, because there had been no time to block off the street.

They recognized the officer—Paul Darden—huddled behind the open door on the driver's side. His gun was trained on the plate-glass windows of the storefront.

Liz and Steve, guns drawn, ran and dropped behind him.

Darden quickly explained the situation. "The manager was able to trip the alarm without the suspect hearing it go off. We pulled up just as he was about to get away. He was coming out the door when we drove up, and he ran back inside and shot the manager. We don't know if he's dead or not. He hasn't fired at us, though. He hasn't done anything but stand there looking scared with his gun at the hostage's head."

It was a small store, the walls lined with shelves filled with bottles of whiskey. There was a short counter to the left, just inside the door, where they could see a man holding a woman in a choke hold. And, as Darden had said, a gun was pressed to her temple.

"Jesus, a woman," Steve said with such misery and despair that Liz paused, despite the pressing situation, to stare at him and wonder what was with him tonight. It was their first active case, and he seemed to be falling apart—the last thing she would have expected of him.

"Give me a minute. Let me think," he said, pressing his thumb against his teeth.

"You do know that he's on parole?" Liz said to Darden.

"Yeah. We heard you guys on the radio just now talking to Bundy."

Steve sucked in a sharp breath, then said, "Okay. We'll wait till his parole officer gets here. He knows him and might be able to reason with him. It's all we can do."

"And if his parole officer can't get him to surrender?" Liz asked, thinking all the while they were wasting time.

"I don't know," he said slowly. "Tear gas, maybe. But we take a chance he'll blow the woman away when the first one pops through the window."

"What you need," Darden said anxiously, "is for a sharpshooter to slip in the back door and get a bead on him so just as the canister flies, he can shoot. Dan Cowley, my partner, is covering back there now. Hell, I wish we had more backup."

Exasperated, Steve said, "Yeah, we need it. Where the hell is everybody, anyway?"

"There was a drive-by shooting in the drug district, plus a big wreck near the Civic Center. Everybody is going crazy. I was hoping once you got here and saw the situation you'd call in the SWAT team."

"We don't have that kind of time. It's bad enough waiting for the parole officer."

Darden argued, "Well, you've got to wait for a sharpshooter, anyway."

"No, we don't," Liz said resolutely. "I can do it."

Steve and Darden stared at her.

"I can," she repeated, looking to Steve for his support. "And you know it."

"No way," he said harshly. "You aren't going in there."

She was adamant. "I have to. I'm the only chance that woman's got. Now get ready to fire the tear gas while I get in position around back."

She scurried into the shadows before he could say anything else. She had agreed he was in charge of the scene, given his experience, and if he had her cited for disobeying an order later, so be it. What counted was trying to save the life of the hostage.

"Hey, you pigs out there…"

She heard Alan Booker's voice through the open door of the liquor store and paused to listen.

"Back off. Back wa-a-a-y off. I'm tired of fooling around."

Steve yelled back, "We need to talk, Booker."

Liz kept on going, knowing Steve was stalling to give her time to get in position, as well as get the tear gas gun ready to fire.

Remembering her training, she called out softly to the other officer before rounding the rear corner of the building. "Cowley, it's Detective Casey. Don't shoot."

"Hey, am I glad for backup," he whispered as she joined him. "But I have to admit I've been hoping he'd come running out that door and give me a chance to waste him. The little punk," he added with a snort.

Quickly, briefly, Liz told him the plan…how she was going in to take position and be ready to fire as soon as they heard the tear gas canister's familiar *whoomp* sound.

"Okay. Go ahead," he urged. "But be careful. If you miss—"

"I won't," she said, knowing she sounded overconfident, but she was a good shot, and it was unlikely she would miss. So, as she eased open the back door and stepped inside, Liz was not worried about succeeding. What did have her in knots was the fear that she would bump into something and make a sound to give herself away, causing Alan Booker to panic and kill the hostage before she could shoot him.

She closed the door behind her and offered a prayer of thanks that it had not squeaked.

She stood there for a moment, blinking against the patrol car's headlights, which were right on the window. It dawned then, with a jolt, that she was going to have a really tough time taking aim in the glare. She also saw that there were boxes in front of her that would prevent a clear shot unless she got around them.

She was about to cautiously move forward when there was a sudden commotion. She heard a curse, followed by two rapid gunshots fired by Booker as he saw someone taking aim with the tear gas gun. Then came the thundering sound of footsteps coming right at her.

She made her move—right into the path of Booker, who slammed right into her, making her drop her gun.

"What the shit—" he roared, then, taking advantage of her surprise, grabbed her in the same choking hold as he'd had on the hostage.

Liz clawed at his arms and kicked her feet, fighting for her breath—her life—as he dragged her down the hall toward the back door.

They were almost there when Officer Cowley appeared. Booker fired, but Cowley leaped back in time to keep from getting hit.

"In here," Booker grunted, spotting the open door to a large storage closet.

He gave Liz a rough shove in front of him that sent her sprawling to the floor, and she watched in terror as he slammed the door and bolted it shut.

"Who the hell are you?" he demanded, face twisted with

furious desperation as he leaned over to press the gun barrel against her forehead.

Liz licked her lips and struggled to keep her voice even, trying to sound brave as she said, "I'm Detective Casey, and shooting me makes you a cop killer. You'll fry for that, Booker."

"You think I care?" He pressed the gun harder.

Liz winced, squeezed her eyes shut, then opened them to plead, "Yeah, I think you do, or you would already have done it. Let's talk about it—"

"Talk about what? About me going back to that stinking prison? No way, baby. I'd rather die."

"No, you wouldn't," Liz argued gently. "You're only twenty years old, right? You'll do some time, but—"

"But with good behavior I'll get paroled, right?" he sneered. "Big deal. I get an asshole for a parole officer who finds me a job making minimum wage and doesn't give a shit when I tell him I want to try for something better. He says I should be grateful for whatever I can get since I'm nothing but scum."

Liz gulped; despite the grave situation she found herself in, she was appalled at what she had just heard. "Your parole officer actually said that?"

"He damn sure did. And me with a family to support."

She felt him pull the gun back a little and dared to hope he was having second thoughts. "But that's not right."

"It's the way it is, baby. So I decided to steal me some money and take my family and hit the road. Only I screwed up big-time, didn't I? And then the woman I was holding up front fainted, and I panicked, but at least those pigs outside missed when they tried to kill me—which is what you were planning to do if you'd been able to sneak up on me, right?" He pressed the barrel against her head again.

Liz knew she had to stay calm and attempt reason or she

was a goner. "Booker, listen. Give yourself up, and I'll do everything I can to help you. The manager—he's not dead, is he?"

"No," he said. "I got him in the leg. I didn't want to kill him—just cause him some pain for triggering the alarm, damn him. I thought I could make it out of here before the cops came, but thanks to him, I didn't."

"So you haven't killed anybody, and all that will happen is you'll do your time and then some. But in a few years, if you toe the line, you'll get a second chance at parole. Think about it," she urged. "A few years, and you'll be out, and I'll try to see that you get a decent parole officer this time. Please, Booker," she begged. "You don't want to kill me. You don't want to go to the electric chair...."

Oh, Lord, she prayed, *let him listen to reason.*

And she silently vowed that she would try to help him...would ask that the situation with his parole officer be investigated. It made her sick to think it might be true. There had been a time when she'd wanted to go into that branch of police work; it had seemed so much more rewarding to help rehabilitate a criminal than catch one. But her father had hit the ceiling when she mentioned it, reciting once again how she was the last hope of carrying on the Casey name in the ranks of police officer.

So here I am, Pop, she thought, trembling from head to toe despite promising herself she never would in such a moment. Here I am, Officer Casey, carrying on family tradition in name only, and you would be really ashamed to see me right now. You'd probably kick yourself for being against me going against tradition and—

"Booker, put down your weapon and come out with your hands up."

"That's my partner," Liz managed to say despite the lump of terror in her throat as Alan Booker's hand jerked.

Glocks were known for going off easy. "Please take that gun away from my head," she begged.

"Booker, don't make it any harder for yourself than it already is," Steve called through the door. "The manager is only wounded. He'll be all right. So will the hostage. But you've got a police officer in there, and it's starting to get serious."

Any other time, Liz might have smiled at the wry remark about starting to get serious, but there was no room for lightness in the midst of soul-wrenching fear.

"Please, Alan," she whispered, hoping she was not just imagining she saw doubt in his eyes. "Please let me go, give yourself up, and I'll do what I said I would. It's your only chance to live."

"I...I don't know." His brow was beaded with perspiration, and he wiped at it with his free hand.

"You said you had a family."

"I...I do."

"How many kids?"

"One...another on the way."

"So what do you think will happen to them if you die? Do you want your kids to grow up having to live with the fact their daddy died in the electric chair? Because you know you aren't going to get out of here, even if you kill me."

"Ah, shit, I don't know."

He spun around, waving his arms over his head, and Liz was just about to muster the bravado to spring for him when he abruptly froze to face her with tears running down his cheeks. "Okay. I'll take a chance you're telling the truth. I don't want to die."

He handed over the gun. Liz grabbed it, and turned him around. Taking handcuffs from her skirt pocket, she fastened them around his wrists.

"Situation secure," she yelled to Steve, lifting her foot to kick the bolt and unlock the door.

It banged against the wall, and he rushed in just as she began to intone to her prisoner, "You have the right to remain silent..."

It was hard to hear what she was saying over the fierce pounding of his heart, and Steve knew in that moment that the hell he had been through in the past moments went far beyond just caring what happened to a partner.

He cared about *her,* damn it, and in a way he had promised himself he never would.

Liz gripped her mug with both hands. Leaning across the booth to speak so no one else in the diner could overhear, she was oblivious to how the steam rising from the hot coffee hit her full in the face. Besides, it was no greater than what had to be coming out of her ears, as mad as she was.

"I can't believe you filed for a reprimand against me, Miller."

Steve matched her glare. "You need reprimanding, Casey. You could have gotten yourself killed."

"No. I did what I thought was best at the time, and I would have succeeded if the hostage had not fainted."

"So he dropped her and grabbed you on the way back." His smile was sardonic. "All because you never should have been there in the first place."

Liz stared into her coffee for a moment, then lifted her gaze to his. "You know what I think? That you've been waiting for a chance to complain about me."

"That's not true, Casey," he lied, then truthfully said, "I'm just worried your recklessness might get you killed one day."

Liz sighed. "I wish I could believe that's all it is."

He felt a stirring and realized he was actually hoping

there was a hidden meaning there somewhere. "Why do you say that?"

"Because I really like working with you, Steve. You're an all-right guy. I've learned a lot from you. But in this instance, I think you were wrong. You know what a good shot I am. I could have picked that guy off with no problem, and if I were a man, you'd have thought so, too. But you had no confidence in me."

"That has nothing to do with it. You agreed I was in charge of the scene, then went against me."

"But I got him to surrender."

He shook his head to remember such a feat. "And I still haven't figured out how you managed to do that."

"I just listened to him—something nobody else seems to have taken the time to do. And I plan to keep my promise to him, too."

"What promise?"

"To help him."

"Help him how?" Steve all but shouted. "By doing what? The guy was out on parole and held up a liquor store, wounded the manager and threatened to kill a customer and a cop. And you want to help him? How? By getting him out on parole again...so he can do it *again?*"

He gave a bitter chuckle and threw his arm across the back of the booth as he stared at her in wonder. "You have got to be kidding, Casey."

"Well, I'm not," she retorted stiffly. "He needs help, and if he had gotten it from his parole officer, he never would have tried to rob that store."

"How do you know that?"

"He told me his parole officer didn't care that he wasn't making enough to support his family, that he was nothing but scum and should be grateful for anything."

"But that's not your area." He rolled his eyes and

sighed. "How do I get through to you without sounding cold? It's just we have a job to do—apprehending criminals, period. It is not our job to try and rehabilitate them."

"Well, I know that," she was quick to concede, "but at the time—"

"Speaking of time—" he glanced at his watch "—we've got to be going."

Doggedly, Liz got up and followed him out.

They were almost to the door when he impulsively put his hand on her shoulder and said, "Please don't take any of this personally, okay? I'm only doing it for your own good."

Liz nodded but was puzzled. He sounded almost too contrite, like maybe *he* was the one taking it personally. Don't go there, she told herself. It's business. Nothing more. Steve Miller saw her as a pesky female officer and that was all. Thinking it might be anything else was asking for trouble...and heartache.

The diner was directly across the street from the police station. They started walking, side by side. Suddenly Steve asked, "What did Tom have to say about it?"

"Tom?" she blinked, then remembered and bit back a smile to think of her cat. The night she made the local news by being a brief hostage at a robbery, Tom had been out doing what he did best—carousing in the neighborhood in search of female companionship.

"Oh, he didn't say much," she said, struggling to keep her voice even and face straight.

Steve's brows rose. "Oh, really? His girlfriend almost gets herself killed, and he's not upset about it?"

"Tom's been busy lately," she said.

"Doing what? You never did tell me what he does for a living. Hell, I really don't know anything about you, Casey, and that's not good, not when we have to count on each other. I need to know what makes you tick.'' Even though I promised myself a thousand times not to give a damn, he thought.

"You don't say much about yourself, either.''

"Nothing to tell.''

They bolted across the street, dodging early-morning Birmingham traffic rather than take the time to go to the corner and wait for the light to change. But then all the officers frequenting the popular diner were guilty of jaywalking.

They reached the other side, and Steve prodded, "So what does he do?''

"Who?''

"Tom.''

Liz had already forgotten the subject. It was hard to carry on a conversation as though her cat were her boyfriend, for heaven's sake.

Just then she saw an enlistment poster for the Navy. The picture presented was a SEAL team in a rubber raft, navigating through rough waters with a caption that read Dare to be different. Dare to be great. Navy SEALs.

"He's a Navy SEAL,'' she blurted. "He's away a lot.''

Steve sneered. "Oh, yeah, well, I can see why he didn't care if you took a risk. That's all those guys know how to do. Was he even in town? Did he see you on TV?''

"He—'' she hedged, trying to figure out what to say that would sound believable "—he was in town, and he saw it, but he didn't say much, like I said, just to be careful. Stuff like that.''

"So where's he stationed?''

She thought of the closest coastal town. "Panama City.'' She did not know if there was a SEAL base there and could only hope Steve didn't, either.

"Then he gets home a lot.''

She glanced at him to think how he actually sounded

disappointed at such a possibility and continued the ruse, "Yes. Yes, he does."

"Well, I guess it keeps you from being lonesome when you're not working."

His tone sounded flippant once more, as though he were merely making conversation and didn't give a rat's fanny what she did when they weren't together. Liz told herself that's how it was supposed to be...how she should want it to be, because the last thing she needed was a schoolgirl crush on a man she could never have. Still, talk of a personal nature had fired her own curiosity, and she decided it was time to find out a few things about him, as well.

"What about you?" she began. "Do you have a—"

They had reached the front door of the precinct and were surprised when it opened abruptly and Walt Rogan impatiently greeted them. "Will you two hurry it up? I want to get this over with. I've got an assignment for you."

It had been a perfect chance to find out about Steve's love life without seeming obvious, but it was ruined. Trying not to look disappointed, Liz followed them into Rogan's office.

Rogan motioned them to sit down, settled behind his desk, shuffled through some papers, then said to Steve, "So tell me what this is all about."

Steve explained what had happened the week before, adding that he would have liked to address it earlier but wanted to take it up only with Rogan and had waited for him to return from vacation.

Rogan looked at Liz. "What have you got to say for yourself?"

Liz explained how she had felt, that, due to her sharp-shooting ability, she had acted properly in volunteering to take the robber down in order to save the hostage.

Turning to Steve, Rogan said, "But you told her to wait for backup."

"I did. She's not an official sharpshooter. I wanted someone who was."

Rogan closed his eyes, thought a moment, then looked at them in turn and said, "Well, I think you both deserve a reprimand."

Steve and Liz cried in unison, "Why?"

"You, Casey, because you disobeyed an order after agreeing Miller was in charge of the scene. And you—" he shifted to Steve "—for not having more confidence in your partner. You've seen her shoot. You knew she was capable. You two are going to have to learn to work as a team and trust each other."

Liz and Steve squirmed uncomfortably in their chairs, grateful when Rogan abruptly changed the subject. "Now let's get back to business. We've had a tip that drugs are being peddled in Rosie's Trailer Park near the bypass. It's supposed to be happening in a yellow trailer all the way in the back. There's a clay bank behind it, so you've got a perfect spot to observe. Rosie, herself, called to report it. Stake it out."

Steve asked, "Isn't Rosie's a place primarily for single women? No men allowed?"

Rogan snickered. "Well, I don't think they're explicitly forbidden, but I pity one who tried to move in there. Mainly it's for single mothers. Rosie Craddock—she's the owner— has made a kind of haven for women having a hard time on their own. That's why she doesn't want drugs in there. Lots of kids. And they've got enough problems without a dealer living right there."

Steve bolted from his chair. "We're on it."

Liz followed him, and they were almost to the door when Rogan called, "You two work things out now, you hear?

You're making a hell of a good team. That's why I'm tearing up your request for a reprimand, Miller. You don't need this between you. As for you, Casey, don't be taking any chances.''

Steve kept on going, and Liz hurried to keep up, wishing things were different, that he would settle down, accept her and that the tension would ease. Because the truth was she felt herself being drawn to him more and more, despite constantly reminding herself she shouldn't be. She found him intelligent, charming and fun to be with—despite his occasional coldness toward her because she was a female officer, but, in time, she hoped that problem would work itself out.

Meanwhile she had to work on hiding how she really felt about him—not as a partner, but as a very desirable male.

They spent the rest of the day scoping out the neighborhood surrounding Rosie's Trailer Park and planning where they would take up their stakeout.

But Liz was not entirely focused on the business at hand. Being with Steve was becoming more and more disconcerting, despite all resolve. Just the masculine nearness of him made her feel a warmth inside she'd not known for ages. She thrilled to the dimple in his cheek when he smiled, the way his eyes twinkled when he laughed, and if he happened to brush against her when they were walking, she reveled in the closeness.

Could it be, she dared wonder, that he might also be feeling drawn to her, as well? There were times when his motive behind urging her to be careful actually seemed more personal than occupational necessity. And more and more lately he seemed to loosen up and put the cop part of him to one side as they enjoyed easy camaraderie.

And he did seem so different from Craig, because she

had begun to suspect that maybe Steve's aversion to women cops stemmed only from the fact that he did not want to personally work with one. And there might be a reason for that, too, she mused, wondering if there might be something in his past that made him feel as he did.

Finally, at dark, they took up their post on the hill looking down on the park illuminated by streetlights.

"I don't like all the kids running around," Steve complained. "Did you notice that even though there's lots of space down there, we didn't see one area set aside for a playground? The kids play in the street, and that's not safe, because there are no speed bumps. And you see those women zipping in and out of there not caring how fast they're going? Sooner or later, they're going to hit somebody."

Steve talked on, but Liz found it difficult to pay much attention to what he was saying. They were sitting on a grassy knoll that overlooked the trailer park, and it was necessary to sit very close so they would blend against the trees behind them and not be noticed. Liz could feel his muscular shoulder pressed against her, and sometimes when he gestured with his hand as he spoke, it would brush against her thigh. She chided herself for feeling like a schoolgirl, but there was no denying he could arouse her with just a touch.

By midnight they were both stiff and sore from their vigil. Liz felt some guilt over not caring...but not much. After all, the discomfort was caused by sitting so close for so long, and she had relished every moment.

They had also achieved their objective by indeed discovering that the woman who lived in the yellow trailer appeared to be selling drugs. Cars came and went, staying but a few moments. In and out the traffickers went, tarrying inside the trailer only long enough for the time it would take to exchange money for narcotics.

"We'll set up a bust tomorrow night," Steve said as they wearily made their way back to where their car was hidden.

"And we can take care of the warrants and all the paperwork in the morning and have it ready," Liz mentioned. "I just hate to think of all she'll be selling between now and then."

"And I hate to think of those kids down there with no place to play, while their mothers are out trying to make a living. Unfortunately, in this section of town, so close to the bypass, there's no park available for them. The school bus drops them off here by three-thirty every afternoon, and they run wild."

Liz, after listening to him for the past few hours, knew he was deeply upset. "I know, but what can you do? Kids all over suffer from living in single-parent homes. It's just a shame these live in an area where there's no recreation area."

Once in the car, Liz was bewildered when Steve drove straight to see Rosie, owner of the trailer park. "You're going to tell her about the planned bust?" she asked, astonished.

"No. She'll find out about that when it happens. I want to talk to her about something else."

Liz trailed behind him to knock on the door of a doublewide. A few seconds later a red-haired woman appeared with a beer in her hand. They had quietly introduced themselves to her earlier, and her eyes went round as she anxiously asked, "Did you see it? Did you see what I told you about?"

Crisply, Steve confirmed, "Yes, ma'am, and we'll take care of it in good time, but there was something else I wanted to talk to you about."

She motioned them inside, and Liz listened as he told Rosie of his complaint about the lack of a play area for the children.

"Well, I agree with you," she said candidly as Steve and Liz sat at her kitchen table having soft drinks while she had another beer. "But I can't afford nothing like that. I cut the rent here to the bone as it is. I barely break even, but that's okay. I don't lose nothing, either.

"But I would," she added defensively, "if I started setting up a park. Where would I get the money for fencing? Equipment? And you say I need speed bumps. I agree with that. I'm always reading somebody the riot act over driving fast, but the city won't pay for them, and I can't afford it."

Steve tapped at his lower lip with his forefinger, a gesture Liz adored.

His lashes dusted his cheeks as he closed his eyes to concentrate, another expression she found appealing.

Finally he said to Rosie, "If I got the money for the playground, would you donate a space for it?"

"Why, of course," she said without hesitation, tears in her eyes. "And God bless you, Detective."

Back in the car, Liz was awed and wasted no time praising Steve herself. "That is real generous of you."

"Oh, I can't afford to pay for it all myself," he said matter-of-factly. "But I believe I can raise the money."

"How do you plan to do that?"

"I'm not sure yet, but it's a worthwhile project, and I think I can drum up some enthusiasm for it. But for now we'd better grab something to eat and call it a night, because we've got paperwork to do in the morning."

They checked in at the precinct, then went to the diner, which was almost deserted at that time of night.

Liz ordered bacon and eggs, but Steve, fired up over the

coming drug bust, as well as the playground project, stoked his enthusiasm with a cheeseburger and fries.

Liz was awed to discover yet another side to Steve she had never known existed—his genuine concern for other people's problems. Craig had been so self-centered, not caring about her wants and needs, much less those of others. Steve, despite the hard, focused cop side of him, was a gentle soul, and Liz was deeply impressed.

When the waitress set his plate down, Liz seized on the chance to turn things personal once more. Pointing at the food, she asked, "Don't you have anybody to cook for you when you get home? I notice you eat out a lot."

He reached for the catsup bottle. "What are you talking about? I know how to cook. I just don't always have the time."

"I'm talking about a significant other. You know, a girlfriend to wait up for you with a snack to hear about your day."

He snickered. "Don't tell me that Tom, your Navy SEAL, is waiting for you with milk and cookies."

"Uh, no..." she stammered, caught off guard as he threw the ball in her court. "But he...he sometimes brings something home."

"So what about you?" She tossed the ball right back.

Steve was having trouble getting the catsup out and punctuated each word with the slap of his hand against the bottom of the bottle. "Oh...she...doesn't...know...how... to...cook."

The catsup came out in a gush, splattering the French fries as well as the table.

"Sorry," he mumbled.

A waitress came running with a towel to clean up the mess, and Liz waited till she was finished before prodding further, "Your friend doesn't cook at all? That's a shame. I'm not very good at it, but I try once in a while."

He took a bite of his cheeseburger and spoke around it, "She doesn't have a lot of time, either."

"Oh, really? What does she do?" Liz chided herself for experiencing a twinge of jealousy to think of the woman who shared Steve Miller's life—and his bed, damn it.

"She doesn't do anything."

"You mean she doesn't work?"

He sipped his Coke, not meeting her eyes. "She's between jobs right now."

"Oh." Liz felt a little bit of mean satisfaction. At least Steve's love interest was not basking in the glory of a successful career...not at the moment, anyway. "What's her name?" she suddenly wanted to know.

Steve was quiet for so long Liz thought he was not going to answer, and then he spoke, so low she had to strain to hear him.

"Mamie," he said almost irritably. "Her name is Mamie."

8

Steve stroked Mamie's ears as she lovingly licked his neck.

For maybe the thousandth time in the past week he wondered how he could ever have made Liz think Mamie was his girlfriend...because Mamie was a dog... A big, cuddly Labrador retriever, and Steve adored her.

When Liz had kept asking him if he had somebody in his life, Mamie was all he could think of—because actually she was all he had. He was not about to admit he didn't have a girlfriend to Liz. If she thought he was on the prowl, she might key in on how he had started feeling about her, and that would never do. So it was best to let her believe he was in a relationship.

But he still felt foolish every time she mentioned Mamie, which she did often, saying things like, "Well, I guess Mamie will be glad we finished early tonight," or "What have you and Mamie got planned for your day off?"

And almost daily she asked if Mamie had found a job yet.

Steve would get away from the subject by asking about Liz's love—Tom—and wondered why she always seemed so reluctant to talk about him. Maybe his being a SEAL and gone so much was a problem. Steve didn't know and told himself it was none of his business. What he needed to concentrate on was getting rid of Liz as his partner, which was starting to look impossible.

He had dared to hope that if he turned in a reprimand request she would have a fit, and Rogan would then come down on her for getting hysterical and decide she was unstable. Instead, she had rolled with the punches and let it go—which had endeared her to him all the more, and Steve didn't need that. He was already attracted to her enough as it was.

Liz Casey, he had decided, had one of the perkiest and cutest personalities he had ever seen in a woman. She took everything in stride, never whined or complained about anything—except him, of course, and then bluntly to his face and not behind his back. She did her part, not asking for special treatment because of her gender. He had seen her take down a guy three times her size with a well-placed karate kick and was intimidated by nothing.

Steve admired her and respected her but only wished he had met her under different circumstances. He even dared hope that when he did get rid of her as his partner that somewhere down the road she might go out with him.

But, he frowned as he thought, they would probably not wind up on friendly terms, because it appeared that in order to accomplish his goal he was going to have to play dirty.

Gently pushing Mamie away, he got up and went into the kitchen for another beer. He knew he was spending too many nights alone in front of the TV, but brooding over Liz kept him from wanting to hang out at the Blue Spot.

He looked at his watch. It wasn't quite eight o'clock. Things would be starting to get lively at the bar. It was Friday night, and he was lucky enough to be off, because there was nothing big going on that couldn't wait till Monday. Sure, he was on call, as always, but he had his beeper on and could be found if needed.

He shoved the beer back in the refrigerator and closed the door, unable to stand another night guzzling in front of the TV. What he needed was female companionship—which he was sure to find at the Blue Spot—to get his mind off Liz. There were always single women hanging out—"uniform groupies," he and the other guys laughingly called them—and some of them were not bad looking.

It was time, he thought with a rush of excitement, to start living again.

And also to stop pining over Liz Casey like a lovesick schoolboy.

He passed the sofa and paused to give Mamie a pat on her head and an apology. "Sorry, old gal, but you'll have to wing it alone tonight, but tomorrow—"

The phone rang.

With a groan Steve dropped beside Mamie.

The only calls he ever got were to report for work, and it wasn't fair for it to happen this night, not when he had made up his mind to do something about his misery.

He stared at the ringing phone. He was tempted to ignore it, then realized he would only get beeped if he did.

Then it dawned.

Why wasn't he getting beeped now?

Always when headquarters wanted to get in touch with him, they would dial his beeper first, and, if he did not respond, they would try to call him at home or on the car phone.

But they always tried the beeper first.

Which meant, he hoped, that it was probably not the precinct calling, after all. Maybe it had something to do with the rummage sale he had planned. He snatched up the phone and answered, "Detective Miller."

"Steve? Hi. I was afraid you'd be out. It's Liz."

His heart went into overdrive, but he managed to sound normal. "So what's up?

"It's about Sunday."

"Sunday?" It didn't register, because his mind was filled with the image of her, picturing rich brown eyes that reminded of warm coffee on a cold morning and hair the color of midnight.

"Yes," she confirmed, sounding perplexed that he could forget something he himself had planned. "The rummage sale, remember?"

"Uh, yeah," he said, thinking of the freckles on the tip of her nose.

Liz laughed. "Earth to Miller. Earth to Miller. Wake up, guy. It's your party. You haven't forgotten about it, have you?"

He drew a sharp breath and told his heart to slow down. "No. Of course I haven't." For weeks, ever since he had discovered the sad situation in Rosie's Trailer Park, he had been working on his idea for a rummage sale to make money for the playground and speed bumps. "So what about it?" He hated to seem brusque, but was anxious to get off the phone and head to the Blue Spot before he changed his mind about going.

Liz, bubbling with enthusiasm, explained, "I got to thinking that homemade baked goods would be a good seller. You know—brownies, cookies, cakes and such. You could ask Mamie to make something, and if we get busy tonight and call some of the guys' wives, I'm sure they'd be glad to help out, too."

"Mamie doesn't bake," he said drily. "As for the rest of the guys, I don't know any of their wives. I'd feel funny calling them about something like that."

"Well, I know them, and I don't mind. I've been around

the precinct for a while, remember? So if you agree with my idea, I'll get busy on the phone.''

"I think it's a great idea, but I'm going to be busy collecting stuff that's been donated, Liz. I'm afraid I won't have time to help you. Can you handle it by yourself?''

"Sure. Just leave it to me, but let's keep our fingers crossed we don't get called out. It's rare that we get to enjoy our days off when they fall on a weekend.''

"Yeah, I know.''

There was a pause, then Liz ventured, "I guess you and Mamie are busy, so I'll let you go...''

"Uh, not really. Is Tom in town?'' he asked, wondering if he would be helping her.

"No, he isn't.''

Her tone was so sharp, he was about to wonder whether there was trouble in paradise when Mamie suddenly gave him a big lick across his face.

"Mamie, no. Stop it,'' he said without thinking, quickly swiping at his wet mouth with the back of his hand.

"Am I interrupting something?'' Liz asked quietly.

Uneasily he said, "No. Mamie's just horsing around. Look, the bake sale is a great idea if you can handle it. Now I'd better go.''

"Yes, it sounds like you'd better.''

She hung up, and so did Steve, but he continued to sit there staring at the phone as he wondered if it was his imagination or if she had really sounded annoyed to think a woman had been kissing him.

"Wishful thinking, Miller,'' he chided himself out loud. "The gal's got a guy. A big, tough Navy SEAL. You're nothing to her but her partner, and that's all you should let her be to you, dummy.''

Mamie licked him again, and he patted her and settled back to click the remote and fire up the TV.

Suddenly he no longer wanted to go to the Blue Spot to try and meet a girl. Talking to Liz had dissolved his enthusiasm, because, no matter how hard he tried to convince himself otherwise, *she* was the one he wanted.

He threw his arm around his dog and pulled her close. "But I guess you're the only girl I've got, Mamie."

She licked him again.

Steve was busy all day Saturday gathering donated articles—bikes, assorted toys, tools, books, even furniture. He was getting lots of cooperation from the others on the force and anticipated making enough money to furnish a playground, as well as have the speed bumps installed.

And all the while he prayed for his beeper to be quiet, lest he get pulled off the project to work a case. If that happened the sale would have to be postponed, because there wasn't anyone else to carry on.

As a courtesy, he tried to phone Liz a few times during the day to see how she was doing with her bake sale but she wasn't home.

He tried again Saturday night, but without luck, and started getting annoyed. Her machine wasn't turned on, so he couldn't leave a message. He didn't want to resort to dialing her beeper. It was understood that only an emergency or call to work would warrant that.

He tried not to think about it but could not help wondering if maybe she was out having a little fling while Tom was away. Steve had not forgotten how funny her voice sounded when he asked if Tom was in town. Maybe she had somebody with her then, and it bothered him to think that could be the case. Liz did not seem the sort to be unfaithful, much less the sort to have lots of boyfriends on the string.

Steve had trouble falling asleep and knew he was going

to have to do something about the situation. Not only was he still adamant that a woman had no business in such a dangerous job, but he was also tired of trying to cope with his feelings for Liz.

After that gut-wrenching night when Alan Booker had held a gun on her inside that closet, Liz had asked him why he had gone completely ballistic when it was all over. He had claimed anger because she had disobeyed him, but of course that really had little to do with it. It was because he had been so worried about her...as well as painfully reminded of another night when he had lost someone he had cared about.

So something was going to have to give—and soon.

At nine o'clock Sunday morning, Steve had everything set up for the rummage sale, but there was no sign of Liz.

The parking lot quickly filled with people, thanks to his being able to get some public service announcements on the radio and an article about the sale in the newspaper.

Items were moving, money was being made, but Steve was getting madder by the minute that Liz had not shown. Rosie came around eleven, which was a blessing, because he needed help with the crowd.

"So where's your partner?" she asked when he persuaded her to stay and work.

"You tell me," he said, sharper than intended.

Rosie cracked, "Hey, don't bite my head off, buddy. I can't help it if she's sleeping in with some guy this morning." She narrowed her eyes and chuckled. "Is that what's got you bent out of shape? Her and some guy?"

At that, Steve bellowed, "Are you crazy? She's my partner. I couldn't get involved with her if I wanted to. And she can sleep with anybody she cares to. I just wish she'd do it when she hasn't promised to help me out."

"Well, she was working real hard yesterday."

"What do you mean?"

Rosie related how Liz had solicited everyone at the trailer park to help out. "She came by last night and picked everything up. I made a batch of brownies, and when she came by to get them, she was all excited over having been able to get so much stuff donated, because it appears the mothers want this playground as much as you do."

"Then where is she?"

"Beats me." Rosie shrugged and went to help a customer.

It was after one when Liz finally appeared. She immediately got to work setting up her tables and carrying boxes from her car.

Steve was in the middle of something and couldn't break away to help her and figured it was just as well, because it gave him a chance to get a grip on himself. Whatever her reason for being late, he had no right to chew her out. Besides, she might guess his real motive—that he was jealous of whoever it was she'd been with.

When he was finally able to go to her, he took one look at a box of melted fudge and declared, exasperated, "Well, that's ruined. Couldn't you get here any earlier?"

She looked close to tears. "I'm sorry. I really am. I guess it just got hot in my car, parked in the sun, but most of the stuff is okay, I think."

Suddenly he knew if he didn't get away from her he might say something he would later regret. The bottom line was that it was none of his damn business what she did. And it had been her idea to gather the baked goods. If she wanted to ruin them by sleeping in with some guy, so be it.

"Steve, wait." She caught him by his sleeve. "I want to tell you why I'm late."

"It doesn't matter," he said, pulling away. "The sale is going okay without you."

He continued walking but could feel her eyes boring into his back and knew she was hurt. Well, so was he, damn it, but for a different reason and one he hoped she never found out about.

The rest of the afternoon passed in a blur to Steve, who felt like a jerk after he'd calmed down and decided he had overreacted.

Finally, when the last customer walked away, and darkness began to fall, and no one was left but the two of them, he went to where she was packing away her things. She had sold out, even the stuff that was melted, and he commended her…and also apologized.

"I guess I was just worried about what could have happened to you. I tried calling all day yesterday and last night, and when Rosie said you'd been by her place to pick stuff up, and you still didn't show up here, I didn't know what to think."

She looked up at him with eyes shining. "Steve, I've got to tell you about it. You won't believe it."

Her expression was so happy he wondered if he wanted to know the reason. If she told him she had got engaged or something he would find it pretty hard to take.

"I finally got to see Alan Booker."

It did not immediately dawn on him who she was talking about.

"You remember him—the parolee who held up the liquor store a few weeks ago."

"You visited him in jail?"

"Yes," she rushed to explain. "But it wasn't easy. I had tried a few times before, but he refused to see me, because he wasn't sure he could trust me. Then last night, after I left Rosie's Trailer Park, I was finally able to get in touch with his wife. I talked to her and made her understand that I sincerely want to help him, so she got him to agree to see me this morning.

"So that's where I've been," she threw her hands skyward in triumph. "And now he's going to file a complaint against his parole officer, because he knows he's got somebody on his side to help him do it."

Steve shook his head in wonder. "I don't believe it."

"I knew you wouldn't," she laughed. "Oh, Steve, I can't begin to tell you how good it feels. When I walked in that visitors' cell, that kid was so down he looked like a flat tire, but now he believes in himself again, and I think it's wonderful."

They were standing behind her car. The trunk was open, and the interior light was the only illumination in the surrounding darkness.

Steve could see how she was glowing with happiness. "I think it's wonderful, too," he said, wishing he had taken time to listen to her earlier so he could have shared her joy instead of acting like such a jerk.

"He's going to prison, of course," she went on to say, "but I think he'll settle down and behave himself and be a whole new person when he gets out. And this time, by golly, he'll receive the right kind of supervision and help he should have had before, because I'm going to do my best to see that he does. So, everything is great," she exulted. "You made a lot of money today, I can tell, and I feel really good about what I did with the baked goods."

Suddenly, without realizing he was going to, Steve kissed her.

It was not a long kiss.

Neither was it a kiss of passion.

He merely wrapped his arms about her, pulled her close

and pressed his lips against hers for the briefest of moments.

When he released her, he felt like a fool, because she was staring up at him, dumbfounded. He also wanted to take her in his arms again and never let her go and told himself he was crazy to think like that. She had someone, damn it, but that did not stop him from wanting her like he had never wanted another woman in his whole life.

"What…what was that for?" she asked in a feathery little voice.

"Uh…" he floundered, stammered, then managed to say, "It's a thank you…for all your help."

He quickly turned away and hurried to finish cleaning up the mess from the rummage sale.

Liz stared after him, shaken to the tips of her toes. Steve Miller, she had decided long ago, just had to be the most perplexing man she had ever encountered.

One minute she was sure he hated her. The next she dared to think he might actually be attracted to her.

And while she was still confused as to his feelings for her, Liz no longer had doubts about hers for him…not after the sweetest kiss she had ever known.

9

Liz had always loved the night. Caressing like soft, black velvet, she felt locked away in a secluded place where she could relish the secret dreams of her heart.

And this night was no different as she relived Steve's kiss and wondered what it had meant.

Gratitude for her help with the rummage sale?

She had to smile at that notion. She had been kissed enough in her life to know it was not a thank-you for brownies.

So maybe, she dared think, he secretly cared about her but had been holding back because he thought she was involved with someone. That would explain why he had seemed so embarrassed afterward.

Tom, curled up at the foot of her bed, rolled over and began making soft purring noises as he snuggled against her feet.

She gave him a nudge. "You may have ruined my love life, you old tomcat. He thinks you're my boyfriend...."

Liz's eyes widened in the darkness as reality struck like the crack of a bat hitting a home run.

Steve had a girlfriend—Mamie.

And Liz reasoned that if he had kissed her for any other reason beyond gratitude he was being unfaithful to Mamie, which seemed unlikely. After all, he spoke fondly of her and seemed crazy about her.

Then, too, with it being against policy for her and Steve to get involved that way, anyway, it was taking a risk, especially right there in the parking lot, where somebody could have been looking out a window, or—

She sat up so quickly it frightened Tom, and, with a howl, he scrambled off the bed to dive under it.

That was it, she thought, fury creeping in. Though it was not a written regulation, fraternizing—which, translated, meant dating—was discouraged in the ranks. Steve, the conniving jerk, knew the easiest way to get rid of her was to have it said they were having a romance, because then they would be split up.

Slamming her head back against the pillow, she cursed out loud, and Tom meowed in protest from his refuge under the bed.

"Oh, the nerve of that creep," she hissed as she threw back the covers.

Switching on the bedside lamp, she got up and began to pad about the room as she raged on. "The miserable, conniving creep. Well, it's not going to happen. I won't let it. And the next time he tries something like that, I'll cool his jets real quick."

Tom slithered out from under the bed and looked at her uncertainly. She reached down and scooped him up to cradle in her arms as she soothed, "It's okay, boy. You're the only man in my life. And the next time that smart-ass tries anything, I'll tell him you'll fix him. He thinks you're a tough Navy SEAL, and—"

Her beeper went off.

She looked at the clock—nearly two in the morning— and felt a chill to know she would not be called at such an hour unless something big was going down.

She grabbed the phone and called in. "It's Casey. What's going on?"

"Detectives have called for backup to help with a stake-out at Vulcan park," the dispatcher told her. "I don't have the details...something about them thinking it might be bigger than they thought it was going to be."

Liz cried, "They wait until two in the morning to decide that? Jeez."

"Hey," he barked back at her, "you got no cause to gripe. You and Miller are the only team to have the weekend off. Everybody else was working, so be glad for what you had."

"Yes, I guess you're right," she conceded. "I'll be there as soon as I can."

"No. Don't come to the station. I've already talked to Miller, and he said to tell you he'll pick you up."

Liz hung up and rushed to get dressed.

Stripping off her sleep T-shirt, she grabbed jeans and a sweatshirt from the closet. When doing regular investigations she dressed in blazer, blouse or turtleneck and skirt, and wore a shoulder holster. Stakeouts were casual. They had to be. One never knew when they'd be called on to pursue on foot or maybe have to engage in hand-to-hand combat.

From her upstairs apartment window, she heard a car driving into the parking lot and knew it had to be Steve.

Stuffing her feet in sneakers, she grabbed up her gun and holster and ran down the steps to yank open the door just as he raised his hand to knock.

"I'm ready," she said, out of breath.

"Then let's go. I'll brief you on the way."

Liz told herself to calm down, because it was not rushing to an assignment that had her pulse tapping. It was anger over Steve's latest ploy to get rid of her that was making her borderline ballistic.

Swallowing against her anger, she listened as Steve explained the situation they were going into. "Mulvaney and Spicer have been staking out Red Mountain the past few nights. That statue up there—"

"Yes, I know. It's Vulcan, god of the forge, made of iron and symbolic of the big iron and steel industry in Birmingham. It's a tourist attraction."

She spoke so woodenly, so curtly, that Steve shot her a querulous glance before continuing, "The narcs got a tip an out-of-town dealer was coming in tonight with some real hard stuff. Mulvaney and Spicer got called in but after they heard the dealer might not be coming in alone, they decided they'd better call for backup.

"Of course," he went on as he turned into the drive leading up to Red Mountain, "the narcs working with them disagreed. They want to be heroes and take all the credit. Mulvaney and Spicer take no chances, so that's where we come in."

"Have you talked to them?" Liz asked.

"Yeah. On the cell phone. The word now is that the meeting is set for three-thirty. The informant seems to be okay. They trust what he's saying. And this could be big. According to Spicer, the dealer coming in is probably responsible for sixty percent of the drugs in Birmingham. Taking him down will be quite a coup."

Liz agreed, then wanted to know, "What's our role?"

"We stake out the south parking lot below the statue. They're expecting the action in the wooded picnic area, so we probably won't see any. We're just a precaution. You'll be safe."

"You don't have to worry about me," she snapped. "I think I've proved I can take care of myself."

"Boy, are you grumpy," he retorted. "I feel sorry for Tom if this is the way you are when you get up."

"I doubt Mamie finds you a joy to live with, either."

He threw his head back and laughed, then said, "Remind me never to call you out at two in the morning."

"You call me whenever I'm needed," she said grimly as she checked her gun. "Even though we both know you don't want to."

"Now just what is that supposed to mean?"

"You know what it means."

"No, I don't."

She gave an airy sniff. "I think you do."

"Are you mad because I said something about Tom?"

"No," she said, then countered. "Are you mad because I said something about Mamie? Maybe you don't want to be reminded of her."

Steve did not speak for several moments, then hesitantly said, "Look, if this has got anything to do with what happened last night…"

Liz had never been the sort to hold anything back for very long, and once he gave her an opening, she let him have it. "It has everything to do with it, because I figured out what you've got in mind, and it's not going to work."

Steve was having difficulty concentrating on maneuvering the car up the curving road, because he kept turning to look at her in astonishment. "What *are* you talking about?"

Staring straight ahead as the car's headlights cut into the soft night she ordinarily loved, Liz said with a sneer of contempt, "You think if you can go to the chief and tell him we're romantically involved, he'll split us up—which is what you've been after from day one." She whipped about to glare at him, eyes burning with rage. "I've tried to overlook it all these weeks—how you've attempted to show me up, make me look foolish. I told myself it was just my imagination—until tonight, when it dawned on me what you were doing. And, God, Steve, that's pretty low,'' she added with a sweep of disgust. ''You ought to be ashamed—coming on to me when I know you're involved with somebody. What do you take me for? You think I hop into the sack with anybody?''

''You've got it all wrong, Liz....''

But there was no more time for talking, as they reached the point where Mulvaney had told Steve to park and rendezvous.

''We'll talk about this later,'' he said, getting out of the car.

Mulvaney had been waiting for them and stepped from the shadows the instant they were out of the car. He gave them their instructions. ''All you've got to do is be ready in case one of them tries to run and heads in your direction.'' He handed Liz a walkie-talkie. ''Use this for communication.''

Tension between Liz and Steve was as thick as the darkness they made their way through to get to their stakeout point. Neither spoke, for silence was imperative as they waited for the dealers to show.

Liz was angry with herself for not holding her temper. She should have waited to say anything, because neither one of them needed to be under more stress than they already were. But she was tired of the charade, tired of him pretending to be her ally, when all he wanted was to see her busted. And for him to take her in his arms and kiss her in an attempt to make it look like there was something between them was the last straw. She would not be surprised if he'd had someone watching, and—

Gunfire exploded the silence.

"This is it," Steve said above the noise. "Let's move out and be ready in case somebody heads this way."

They stepped from their cover in the bushes, but neither saw the man running toward them until he crashed right into Steve.

Caught off guard, Steve was thrown back against a picnic table and suffered a swift kick in the groin from the fleeing drug dealer that left him crumpled and gasping for breath.

Liz had her gun drawn and yelled at the retreating figure, "Stop or I'll shoot."

He kept on going, but Liz did not fire. She was not privy to information as to where all the narcs were posted and was not about to risk firing at the bad guy and hitting a good guy instead.

There was scant moonlight, and she could barely make him out but had an edge in knowing which direction he was headed, because she knew the area well, having lived nearby when she first moved to Birmingham. The fleeing suspect was going straight toward a row of bushes that bordered the concrete parking lot of a local TV station.

Slowing from a run to a fast pace and careful to watch out for hulking shadows indicating trash cans or benches, she pulled her walkie-talkie from where it was clipped to her belt. "This is Casey," she spoke into it. "Is anybody staked out in the parking lot of the TV station?"

A voice came back. "This is Bowden. I'm in the rear of the lot."

"Well, get around to the front as quick as you can, because you've got a bad guy coming straight at you, Bowden."

"I'm on my way. What's going on up there?"

"I have no idea. We heard gunfire and came out of hiding. Miller got kicked, and I was in pursuit, but there's no need for me to break my neck, too, so I'll pass the bad guy on to you."

"What are you talking about? I'm in front now, by the way."

She smiled to inform him, "Well, in about ten seconds he's going to go crashing through those azalea bushes and land right in your lap—"

"Oh, yeah," Bowden cried jubilantly, "he's here."

Liz could hear a yelp of pain in the background and what sounded like a series of thumps.

Bowden left the walkie-talkie on, and Liz could hear the bad guy whining that his ankle was broken. Then there was the clicking sound of handcuffs. Bowden read him his rights, then remembered her and said, "Situation secure here, Casey. Go see to your partner."

When she got back to where she had left Steve, he was sitting up on the bench that had tripped him. He'd had his wind knocked out but was almost fully recovered and able to walk with her back to where the others were gathered near the statue.

No officers had been wounded, but one of the dealers was dead, and three of his men had been injured. The element of surprise had worked, and Liz was pleased to know that for a while, anyway, much of Birmingham's drug supply was cut off.

Bowden came driving up with his prisoner in the back seat of his car. Spotting Liz, he yelled out to her, "Good work, Casey. If you hadn't warned me he was coming my way I'd have lost him."

Everyone congratulated Liz for her quick thinking.

Mulvaney asked how she knew where the bad guy was headed, and she told him.

Then, for some strange reason she did not understand,

she felt the need to dim some of the shine by saying, "He wouldn't have gotten away. His ankle was broken."

Bowden laughed. "The hell it was. He was just trying to fake me off, get me to check it out so he could get the jump on me. There's nothing wrong with him. You did good, Casey." He slapped her on the back.

Aware of how Steve was watching with a deeply thoughtful expression, Liz quickly said, "No, *we* did good—all of us," and raised her hand for a high-five.

Liz noticed that Steve took his time getting in the car, breezily chatting with fellow detectives. She waited patiently, aware that every so often his gaze would briefly, pensively, shift to her.

When the scene was finally cleared, and they got in the car to leave, Steve did not turn toward the main road out. Instead he drove to a lookout point favored by dating couples for the romantic view of Birmingham by night. At four in the morning, however, it was deserted.

"What are we stopping here for?" Liz asked uneasily as he positioned the car above a carpet made of thousands of twinkling lights.

Switching off the engine, he swiveled in his seat to look at her in the mellow glow. "Because we need to talk, Liz. I haven't been able to think of anything else since you said what you did back there about me kissing you last night. I think that's why that guy was able to take me down—I wasn't alert as I should have been."

She sat stiffly, arms folded across her chest, and stared straight ahead.

"Do you really think I did it to try to get us involved so they'd break up our team?" he asked.

Lifting her chin, she countered, "What other reason would you have?"

His chuckle was soft and provocative, causing her to turn

sharply to stare in wonder that he could laugh at such a time.

But in a flash he became somber, and, in that crystalized moment when their gazes were transfixed, he whispered, "What reason, indeed, Liz? I did it because I wanted to...like now."

He reached out and pulled her into his arms, and Liz felt herself yielding like a willow in a windstorm, even though a part of her was screaming to push him away, reject him, chastise him, curse, yell, do anything but listen to the other voice within—the voice coming from her heart, urging her to surrender.

Cupping her face with a warm, caressing hand, his lips feathered over her mouth, teasing, making her yearn for more.

She moaned softly, deliciously, as she twined her arms about his neck and leaned into his embrace.

"I would never do anything to hurt you," he murmured. "You must believe me, Liz. Why do you think I was so mad after that jerk took you hostage in the liquor store? I was afraid for you...I've always been afraid for you. You're so delicate and sweet..."

Liz had difficulty framing her words, because her heart was racing like crazy, and she thought if he did not go ahead and kiss her she was going to explode. Even if he was scheming to get rid of her...even if he did belong to someone else, there would be time later for regrets. But this was here and now, and she could no longer lie to herself. She was falling in love with Steve Miller, and she wanted his kiss more than she had ever wanted anything in her life.

At last his mouth pressed harder, his tongue slipping between her lips. She met it with her own, reveling in the sensation as they pressed yet closer.

For long, tender moments he seemed to devour her with

the seeking, claiming kiss, and Liz could only melt against him, rivers of pleasure coursing through her veins.

His hand slipped to her breast to caress and squeeze, then dived beneath to move nimble fingers inside her bra. He rubbed at her nipple, which was already hard and throbbing and begging for more.

"I want you, Liz," he lifted his lips to whisper. "I don't care about rules and regulations. I want you..."

That resisting part of her started up again as his fingers dropped to the zipper of her jeans.

What if he really was out to get rid of her? she wondered dizzily, frantically. If he had been trying to make her look incompetent, he had failed. Maybe he figured this was all that was left—to fraternize.

Then the surrendering side of her argued that if that was the case, so what? She would know the momentary joy of making love with the man she had come to unconditionally love in the weeks they had been together. And if this was the only night they would ever have, then so be it. She would have the sweet memories, which could often overshadow bitter regrets.

Pressing her back in the seat, her legs were stretched out, and he was able to easily slide down her zipper.

"Maybe we should get in the back seat," he said as he began to fumble with his own jeans. "This is kind of awkward, and—"

Suddenly a light flashed across the window as a voice boomed, "All right, you kids. Move on. You've got no business here this time of night...."

"Patrol car," Steve whispered in a frenzy as he quickly sat up.

"Move on now," the officer yelled, slowly driving on by.

Liz zipped her jeans and sat up to worriedly ask, "Do you think he recognized you or the car?"

"No," he said grumpily. "He didn't get a good enough look to tell it's an unmarked cruiser. But he picked a hell of a time to do a job he should've been doing before now, and maybe we wouldn't have had this drug problem."

Liz, feeling awkward, said, "Well, they can't be everywhere. I know—I used to be in patrol."

Steve started the car. "Well, we'd better get going, or he'll be back."

Neither spoke until they were off Red Mountain, then Steve started to say something, but Liz cut him off. Second thoughts had taken over the desire that had burned so brightly only moments before. "Look, maybe we should split up. I mean, this isn't right, and we both know it."

"Why isn't it right?" he argued. "Look, Liz, we're mature adults. We know what we're doing. Lots of couples working together have relationships. If they get found out, they just transfer them to other teams, other precincts. And I hope by now you realize I don't want that. But it's not a big deal. If it were, it would be spelled out in the procedures manual, wouldn't it?"

She was quiet for a moment, then soberly said, "Well, there's another rule not written in any book that I know of, but it's still there."

"What rule?"

"The one about commitment. I'd say you've got one with Mamie, wouldn't you?"

She did not see Steve's painful grimace.

"Yeah," he said finally, tempted to tell her the truth but knowing it didn't matter, anyway. "And you've got one with Tom."

"That's right." She nearly choked on the lie, but what difference did it make? At least it gave her an illusion of pride. "So let's just forget it happened and go on from here, okay?" She tried to make her tone light.

Steve also forced brightness he did not feel. "Sure. I guess it was the atmosphere up there—made me feel like a horny teenager again. What say we stop and have some breakfast?"

Liz knew the best thing she could do for herself right then was get away from him as fast as possible so she could reason and rationalize away her impulsiveness in yielding so easily to the passionate moment.

"I don't think so," she said with the biggest smile she could muster. "You might be surprised and find Mamie's got your breakfast ready and waiting."

Steve thought about the big, lazy Labrador who had probably leaped into his bed to curl up on his pillow the minute he'd left the apartment.

"Yeah," he muttered, hating himself again for the lie. "I'd be really surprised if that happened."

10

Liz had never dreamed it could be so hard to pretend not to be in love with somebody.

In the days and nights that followed the incident on Red Mountain, she was all business with Steve. No personal talk. No camaraderie. She was a detective, doing her job.

He had attempted only once to talk about it, saying he just wanted to make sure she understood he'd had no ulterior motives.

She had assured him there was no problem, that it was in the past and best forgotten.

The tension, however, was unbelievable, and Liz began to appreciate why romantic involvement between officers was discouraged. It just created too much diversion, when the focus should be on work.

She began to wonder if she should ask for a transfer, but nixed that idea after worrying it might be said she and Steve did not get along, and that wouldn't look good for either one of them.

She hadn't been a detective long enough to request anything, anyway. Technically, she was still on probation, and a major goof could send her straight back to patrol. So there was nothing to do but put on a good front and go forward.

Standing at the kitchen sink, she was cutting up lettuce

for a salad. Tom brushed against her leg and gave a very bored-sounding meow.

"I know," she told him. "I'm bored, too." It was that way whenever she had a night off, but thank goodness they didn't come around too often. Detectives were, of course, on call twenty-four hours a day, and she hungered for the work to stay busy. The downer was that she stayed busy with the person who caused the lonely feelings when she wasn't.

The phone rang, and Liz felt a rush, then reminded herself if it was a call to work, she would have been beeped instead.

Wiping her hands on a paper towel, she hurried to answer and heard her father's cheery voice on the line. "How's my girl? Are they calling you Dirty Liz, yet?"

She groaned and wondered if people ever compared detectives to anyone besides Clint Eastwood's role in his Dirty Harry movies. "No, Pop, and I hope they don't. Harry went around killing people all the time. I pray I never have to."

"Oh, I'm just kidding," he said, and laughed.

But she knew he wasn't. He was a hard-nosed cop through and through, and nothing fazed him. She could remember when he had shot and killed someone in the line of duty. He had shown remorse for having to do it but bore no scars for taking a human life. So sometimes Liz wondered if she had what it took to be a cop, after all, or at least the kind her father wanted her to be.

"How are things going?" he wanted to know.

"Fine, fine," she assured.

"Any collars lately?"

Collar was a slang term for an arrest credited to an officer, and Liz said she had made a couple but nothing dramatic. She told him a little about the chase at Red Mountain, and he said he was proud of her for thinking on her feet, adding, "But that's what being a good cop is all about, right? Say," he rushed on, "I've been thinking—that slick L.A. detective isn't trying to push you into the background to make himself look good, is he? I figured you'd wind up with a man partner, but I worried when I heard he was from California. Out there they consider us hick cops."

"Oh, Pop, they do not," she laughed. "You don't trust anybody outside the South, so it wouldn't matter where he came from if it wasn't below the Mason-Dixon line. You'd still be suspicious."

"Probably," he admitted. "But I don't want you letting him push you around, you hear? And this is why I wanted you to stay and join the force here in Montgomery, honey. I could have made sure nobody tried to walk all over you."

"Which is precisely why I didn't stay there, because I want to make it on my own, not because I'm Sergeant Bill Casey's little girl."

"Well, I would've been proud. I still am, though, and you know it."

They chatted on, talking about plans for Thanksgiving which wasn't far off. Liz could not promise to make it home, even though it was only an hour or so drive from Birmingham. Her father understood she was never able to commit herself till the last possible moment.

Hearing the call-waiting beep, she cut him short. "Sorry, Pop. I've got a call coming in. It might be headquarters, so I'd better take it."

"Sure you do. Now you come home when you can. We miss you, and Mom sends her love. And be careful," he said, which was his stock phrase for ending a conversation.

She assured him she would, hung up and held her breath as she waited for the phone to ring, then told herself she was being silly to get excited. Steve would not phone. Why should he? And she was wrong to even want him to. He had someone, damn it. How long did she have to keep reminding herself of that fact?

The phone rang, and she answered right away, scolding herself to hope it was Steve, anyway, and that they were being called out. Investigation or stakeout was better than a night alone listening to Tom purr, she thought with an apologetic glance in his direction.

"Liz? Hi. What're you doing?"

It was Carol, and Liz swallowed a sigh of disappointment. "Fixing supper."

"Well, save it for another day and meet me at the Blue Spot. There's a new guy on patrol I'm after, and I don't want to look obvious by going there alone."

"Sorry. You're on your own. I'm tired, and nothing is going to drag me out tonight short of being called out on an emergency."

"Which wouldn't be so bad," Carol said, laughing, "not when you're working with 'The Hunk.'"

"Are you girls still calling him that?"

"Yep, but since we heard the rumor about him carrying a torch for somebody back in L.A., we've given up hoping any of us had a chance."

Liz frowned. "I think you've got it wrong. He has somebody here."

"Really? Are you sure?"

"That's what he told me. Her name is Mamie, and I get the impression they're living together."

"Well, you must be the only person who knows that," Carol said in wonder. "The times I've seen him at the Blue Spot—which isn't often—he's never had a girl with him."

"I think Mamie is a bit strange," Liz confided. "She doesn't work, doesn't cook, and I've never heard him say they go anywhere or do anything together. In fact, he never even mentions her unless I do.''

''Hmmm. That is weird,'' Carol agreed. ''Oh, well. It must be nice working with a good-looking guy like that, anyway. Is he treating you okay? I remember you said in the beginning he was a woman hater.''

''I think he'd prefer a man for a partner, yes, but I have no complaints. We get along well together.''

''I'm glad to hear it.''

''But tell me,'' Liz asked, curiosity prodding her, ''what exactly did you hear about him having a girl in California?''

''Well, you know personnel files are highly confidential, but somebody said they heard he left because of a woman.''

''That's all?''

''Afraid so, but there's probably nothing to it if he told you he's involved with somebody. Now—'' she drew an excited breath ''—let me tell you about Wayne. He is absolutely the most—''

The call-waiting beep sounded again and Liz quickly said, ''Sorry. Got a call. Talk to you later,'' and hung up. She supposed she should have put her on hold, but the truth was she didn't feel like listening to Carol blather about her newest interest, which would, no doubt, be followed by endless pleas to go with her to the Blue Spot.

The phone rang, and Liz hit the button, said hello, and instantly froze to hear Steve's voice. ''Hi. I was afraid I'd get your Navy SEAL and he'd want to punch my lights out for calling.''

''Uh, no,'' she stammered, frantically trying to gather her wits, because she had been caught off guard. ''He…he wouldn't mind.''

''That's good. What are you two doing tonight?''

Dear Lord, she thought with a shiver, surely he wasn't

going to invite her and Tom over for an evening with him and Mamie.

She looked at Tom. He was curled up on the rug next to the back door. "Uh, he...he's asleep," she stammered again. "He's tired. Some kind of exercise the SEALs had last week. He just got home. He...he's tired," she repeated, then stamped her foot in exasperation at herself for sounding so out of control.

Tom jumped when she stomped, and, with an angry screech, ran out of the room.

"What's that?"

"Cat," she all but whispered, then, swallowing hard, asked, "So, what's up?"

"I've got a report I need you to sign with me, and I'd like to turn it in tomorrow morning first thing."

"But we're off tomorrow."

"I know, but it needs doing."

She also reminded him, "And we're off tonight, which is precious and rare. So why spoil it with work?"

"Because—" he drew a deep breath and let it out before admitting "—it should've already been done."

She laughed. "Aha. So, because you didn't get your work done on time, you want me, on my night off, to help you out. Know what I ought to do?" she teased. "Hang up the phone, turn off the lights, not answer the door and let you stew, to teach you a lesson."

"Do that," he feigned an ominous tone, "and the next time we do a bust, I won't get in the way of a bullet aiming for you."

She laughed. "First of all, I'd have to get in the way of a bullet to get blown away, and I try not to let that happen. Second, you'd never do that, and you know it, so stop bluffing."

He growled into the phone. "I'll find a way to get even.

And don't think I'm scared of your tough Navy SEAL, either.''

The reminder of her lie was sobering, and suddenly Liz wanted to end the conversation, do what he was asking and then go back to trying not to think about him, blast it. "Okay. I'll meet you out front in fifteen minutes. Don't blow the horn if you get there first. You'll annoy the neighbors.''

"And Tom,'' he added, making a wooing noise like he was scared. "Let's not upset the tough guy.''

Liz put the phone down and started upstairs, but the cat gave her a start as he bolted from beneath the sofa to run in front of her. "You big fur ball,'' she grumbled, following him up the steps, "you cause problems you don't even know about.''

Ten minutes later, Liz stepped outside her front door wearing navy sweats emblazoned with the letters BPD, for Birmingham Police Department.

She was surprised to find Steve waiting.

He met her at the curb. "We can do it in my car. It won't take but a minute.''

"Whatever.''

Inside the car, he used a flashlight to show her the report, which was routine, but, as he'd said, long overdue. He handed her a pen, she scrawled her name under his, and that was it.

"Okay,'' she said quickly, anxiously. "I'd best get back in.''

He caught her arm and held it. "Can you stay just a minute longer? I'd really like to talk to you, Liz.''

Unease began to creep. "What about?''

"I think you know.''

She tensed. "If it's about what happened at Red Mountain, like I said before, we've just got to forget it, because it shouldn't have happened.''

"Maybe you feel that way, but I want you to know I don't have any regrets.''

The porch light cast enough light that she could see his face, could see how his brow was furrowed and his eyes clouded with despair.

As soft as gossamer lace in a summer breeze, she timorously chided, "You should have, Steve. It was wrong." She gathered her wits and, feeling stronger, said, "We have to quit talking about it. If we don't, you leave me no choice but to request a transfer, and I don't want to start talk by doing that, but I will if this keeps up."

He had been turned in the seat, facing her, but twisted around to throw his head back and groan, "How in hell did I ever get to this point after all the promises I made to myself?"

"What are you talking about?"

Steve wished he had left well enough alone, wished he could have been strong enough to let it go. But if there were any chance at all that she might care about him...if maybe she wasn't completely happy with Tom—which he wondered about after she had yielded so easily to his kisses—then he needed to know it. And she also needed to know that the only woman living with him had four legs, big feet and a cold, wet nose.

Liz put her hand on the door handle. "I think I'd better go inside."

He grabbed her arm again. "No, wait, please. I've got a confession to make."

Quickly, frantically, he rolled over in his mind once more the explanation he had rehearsed again and again, how he would admit to the lie about Mamie by saying he wanted

Liz to think he had somebody, too, so she wouldn't think he had any designs on her.

But he had put a crack in that safe harbor, he cursed to recall, by kissing her in the parking lot after the rummage sale, and then he'd gone on to blow it all to hell by trying to make love to her in the parking lot on Red Mountain.

Even more ridiculous—which he was not about to admit—was how he had allowed things to get so out of hand after putting so much energy, in the beginning, to getting rid of her.

Steve Miller, he admonished himself, you're the quintessential fool when it comes to women.

"I don't like the way this is going," Liz said tightly, jerking from his grasp.

"Hear me out, please. I want to tell you about Mamie. It's not what you think."

Liz told her heart to slow down, because even if he and his lover were having problems, she didn't want him on the rebound. "I'd rather not hear about it, Steve. We agreed to keep our relationship professional, and—"

"Yeah, maybe you're right." He slumped back in the seat again. What was the point in setting the record straight if she didn't give a damn about him and never would? "You've got Tom. You don't need anybody else in your life."

Liz sat up straight. "And what is that supposed to mean?"

He shrugged. "You're in love. You don't care about anybody else. I was a fool to think you might care about me."

She blinked, shook her head, swallowed hard and gave up on her heart. If radar had a bead on it, the needle would blow off the scale. "You...you mean that's what this is all about? But Mamie—"

"To heck with Mamie. She's not my girlfriend."

"She...she isn't?" Liz asked, hope creeping.

"Hell, no. I'll explain about her later, but right now I want to know about you and Tom, how serious you are about him. I mean, you might not like hearing it, but I got the impression the other night you weren't exactly kissing me like a woman who's in love with another guy."

Liz giggled.

She couldn't help it.

Because carrying on a conversation about a scruffy old tomcat was suddenly too much.

She began to laugh and couldn't stop, and soon tears were rolling down her cheeks, and Steve was looking at her like she had lost her mind.

Finally, when she could get hold of herself, Liz opened the car door and motioned for him to follow. "Come on. I think it's time you met Tom."

He held up his hands in surrender as though someone had the drop on him. "Hey, wait a minute. I don't know what you think is so damn funny, but let's leave him out of it. I've obviously made an even bigger fool of myself than I thought, so maybe *I'd* better be the one to ask for a transfer."

He reached to turn the ignition switch.

Liz leaned back inside the car. "Please," she said quietly, no longer laughing. "Come with me. I'd rather show you than tell you, and then, believe me, *I'll* be the one who feels like a fool—not you."

Doggedly, he got out and trailed after her. "I don't see what meeting your boyfriend has to do with your answering my question about how serious things are. And I'd only planned to tell you about Mamie, anyway, and how she's not my girlfriend. She's my—"

"You can tell me later," Liz said as she opened the front door, trembling to think how, if he did care about her, and

Mamie really didn't mean anything to him, there might be a chance for them, after all.

But first he had to learn the truth about Tom.

She glanced around the living room, then looked in the kitchen and finally pointed to the stairs. "He's up there. Probably under the bed."

Steve wasn't sure he had heard her right. "Did you say what I think you said?"

"I did."

"Mind telling me what he's doing under there?"

She hoped he was not going to be mad when he learned the truth. "You'll have to ask him."

"Look, you said he was just tired. If he's under the bed, he's got to be drunk, and I'd rather meet him when he's sober."

"Oh, he's sober," she assured him with a mysterious smile.

"So I repeat—what's he doing under the bed?"

"He likes to sleep there. Now come on."

With a loud sigh, he followed her up the stairs. "This is getting weird."

She switched on the bedroom light. The bed was neatly made. There was no sign of Tom.

She pointed under the bed. "He's under there, like I thought."

Steve threw his arms up in exasperation and turned toward the door. "That does it. I'm out of here."

"No, wait, please." She dropped to her knees and pulled up the spread. "Tom, come out from under there. I want you to meet somebody."

"I'm gone..." Steve yelled, bolting for the door.

"Here he comes."

Curious to see the kind of guy who preferred to sleep

under a bed instead of on it, Steve stepped back for one quick look.

A big yellow cat crawled out to yawn, then fixed him with an annoyed stare.

"This," Liz said with a guilty look, "is Tom."

"Wh-what are you talking about?" Steve stammered, cautiously stepping back into the room. "You...you mean that cat—"

She nodded.

He gulped and swallowed, his voice suddenly failing him as he struggled to comprehend the situation. Then, finally, he whispered, "You mean Tom never existed? You just made him up?"

"Not exactly. There is a Tom. This is him. Carol started it all that night at the Blue Spot when she was trying to play Cupid and wanting to make you jealous. And I'm afraid I played along to make you think I had somebody and wouldn't be coming on to you."

He leaned over to pat Tom on the head, but the cat arched his back, spit at him and ran back under the bed.

Liz grinned. "He's not used to having other men in the bedroom."

Steve, overcome to realize what it all meant, murmured, "I'm glad," and reached for her.

But Liz quickly raised her hands to fend him off, not about to let things go any further till she had a few answers of her own. "I think we'd better go downstairs and have a cup of coffee. It's time to clear the air between us completely, and I want to hear all about Mamie."

He reached for her hand. "No, I've got a better idea. I think it's time you met her."

11

Her stomach muscles were twisting as Liz said, "I'm not so sure this is a good idea. Maybe we'd better do it another time, like during the day. I mean—what if she's gone to bed, and we wake her up?"

Steve's mouth twitched, wanting to smile. Mamie would definitely be asleep. "Nothing to worry about. She always gets up when I come home."

Liz laced her fingers together and squeezed. "I still think we should wait."

"No. It has to be tonight. You have to know the truth about Mamie."

"But...but if she's not your girlfriend, why did you let me think that?"

He pulled into the parking lot of his apartment complex. "Maybe my motive was the same as yours," he said thickly.

Liz felt her cheeks grow warm.

"Come on upstairs," he urged, gliding the car into the space with "Miller" stenciled on the concrete bar directly in front of it. "Just don't pay any attention to the mess. I'm a bachelor, remember?"

Liz couldn't help thinking how if Mamie were sharing his place she could at least help out with the cleaning but was not about to say so.

The complex was much like her own—four units in a building, two up, two down. She envied Steve's location at the very back, upstairs and away from traffic and quiet for day sleeping when he had to work all night.

As they started up, Liz noted his apartment was dark and whispered, "This is crazy. I don't want to wake up a woman I've never met just so you she can tell me she isn't your live-in lover, for crying out loud. So let's go somewhere and have a burger and forget about it for now.... I'll pay," she added to entice him.

A yellow porch light showed the way.

Steve's key ring jingled in his hand.

She protested again, "I just don't think—"

"We're here." He fitted the key in the lock, turned it, then snaked his hand inside to punch in the code number to disengage the security system.

"See?" Liz poked his side. "She's even got the alarm system on. She's dead to the world, and she's not going to appreciate us barging in like this, and—"

He had just shoved the door open. Light from the porch spilled into the room, and Liz froze in terror to see a huge shadow leap at Steve. Her first horrified thought was that, despite the alarm system, they had caught an intruder, and he was attacking. Instinct made her reach for her gun, then she remembered that Steve had hustled her out of her apartment so fast she had stupidly forgot to strap on her holster. Breaking from her frozen stupor, she screamed, "Look out!" and rushed to his help.

Steve tried to explain what was happening, but it was too late. Her arms went about the big, black dog, and they both went crashing to the floor.

Liz screamed to find herself grappling with what she thought was a wild, hairy animal of some sort that had somehow found its way into Steve's apartment.

Steve kicked the door shut in hopes the neighbors hadn't heard and reached for the switch to flood the room with light.

Liz and Mamie were still rolling on the floor, with Mamie, a gentle old soul, whimpering in terror and trying to coax Liz into backing off by frantically licking her face.

Liz's eyes went even wider to realize she was holding a very frightened dog and gave a quick and mighty shove as she screeched, "What is going on here?"

Scrambling to her feet, she whirled on Steve, who had convulsed with laughter and was leaning across the back of the sofa to keep from falling down.

Liz exploded. "That dog attacked me, and you think it's funny? What is wrong with you?"

Mamie bolted up and ran to the sofa in search of refuge in Steve's arms. Still laughing, he embraced her as he tried to explain to Liz, "*You* attacked *her*. This is Mamie, and she wouldn't hurt anybody for the world."

Liz shook her head. "You're kidding."

"No, I'm not. I've had her since she was a puppy."

"And you let me think she's your girlfriend?" Liz stared in disbelief. "But why?"

"The same reason you let me think Tom was your boyfriend."

Liz gave the big, black dog an apologetic pat. "I don't know what to say."

"Now you know how I felt when you introduced me to your cat." He started towards the kitchen. "I'll get her a biscuit, then she'll settle down, and we can talk."

Liz looked around the room. The walls were white with miniblinds at the windows. There was a plaid sofa, a recliner, big-screen TV, VCR and a CD player. It definitely smacked of being inhabited by a single guy.

Beer cans littered the end tables. Sports magazines and

newspapers were scattered about. An empty pizza box was on the coffee table.

Through an open door, she could see the bedroom and was surprised to note the double bed was neatly made.

Steve came out of the kitchen carrying two glasses and a bottle of wine. Mamie, a big dog biscuit in her mouth, padded along behind him but turned and went into the bedroom.

Liz's grin was sheepish. "She sleeps under the bed, too, huh?"

"No. She has her own bed." He poured the wine, handed her a glass, then held his up in a toast. "I think we need to drink to a new beginning."

She clicked her glass to his. "Hear, hear. I'll drink to that."

They took a sip, then Liz sat down on the sofa while Steve exchanged the overhead glare for soft lamplight before joining her.

Liz tucked her legs beneath her and stared at him thoughtfully over the rim of her glass as she took another sip, then said, "We're silly, you know it? To think we actually did something so stupid, so that neither of us would think the other was available."

"Not only that," Steve added, "we each thought the other was being unfaithful."

Suddenly Liz found herself in an awkward situation, being alone with someone she was deeply attracted to—who had also confessed to feeling likewise about her. "I think," she said, placing her glass on the coffee table, "that we should talk about this another time. It's late, so if you'd drive me home..."

She started to get up, but he caught her hand. "Stay, please. I think we need to be together. I think we need—" he moved closer "—this...."

He kissed her, and for an instant she held back, fighting a battle within herself between yielding and running. But then a strong, passionate voice within told her she didn't have to run. There was nothing wrong in yearning for someone…wanting someone. And she had a right to happiness, to joy.

But what about tomorrow? a dissenting voice countered. *What if you have regrets?*

Life, Liz told herself fiercely, was filled with regrets. And when those regrets replaced dreams, it was time to take stock. What about those dreams she'd once had, and had dared to think might actually come true?

What about loving Steve Miller and being loved in return?

And, with that warm thought of comfort, Liz surrendered herself to him…body and soul.

Her lips parted beneath his, allowing his tongue to enter her mouth and meld with her own. His fingertips, cupping her face, moved to trace tiny little circles in the hollow beneath her ear, which sent burning tingles soaring through her body.

Slowly, ever so slowly, he trailed them down her throat. She felt a quickening as his mouth followed, and a faint moan escaped her as her primal need awakened and begged to be fed.

Deftly, Steve drew her into the rolling currents of passion, driven by the heated throbs of his own body.

Slowly, ever so slowly, he maneuvered his fingers beneath her sweatshirt to unfasten her bra, then swiftly moved to free her breasts and close his hands around both of them.

She leaned into him as he cupped and squeezed, and she moved her hands to caress first his shoulders, then boldly drop to his chest. He was also wearing a thick sweatshirt, which she dived beneath to run her fingertips through the thick mat of chest hair, then gasped to realize his nipples were taut with eagerness like her own.

"I think I've wanted this from the day we met," he confessed, raising his head to gaze down at her in fiery adoration. "Only I didn't know it then. It took your nearly getting killed to make me realize how much I do care about you, Liz. But thanks to the lie I'd told—and believing you had somebody—there was nothing I could do about it."

"Till Red Mountain," she teased, touching his nose with a loving fingertip as she smiled up at him.

"And we've worried about it ever since." Gently he pressed her back on the sofa, his hand lowering to the zipper of her jeans. "But no more, my darling. No more..."

They helped each other strip off their clothes, and Liz abandoned any shyness or reserve she might have had, as she unleashed her emotions. She danced her fingers along the muscular shoulders and arms she had found so appealing for so long, then boldly dived to cup the tight, firm buttocks that had ignited lusty stirrings with stolen glances.

Flesh to flesh, they twined together. Steve's mouth feasted upon hers while his hands explored between her legs.

Liz felt electrifying bolts of pleasure coursing through her loins and arched against his probing finger.

Feeling his hardness against her thigh, her hand, with a will of its own, dived downward to skim the length of it, then squeeze and draw him toward her. And in that heated moment of desire unlike anything she had ever known before, Liz felt she would surely die if he did not take her then and there.

"I want you," she whispered arduously. "Take me, Steve, please..."

"And I want you, my darling." Trembling with hunger, his mouth claimed her breasts, lips nibbling upon the tender, soft flesh. He fastened about her nipple and bit ever so gently.

Liz moaned in sweet anguish and began to writhe beneath him. Leaving the caressing of his swollen shaft, she caught his head in her hands and held him against her bosom, back arching to render herself to him. His mouth was hot and hungry, and she ached to give him as much of herself as she could.

Steve continued to take delight with each breast in turn, rolling her nipples between his teeth, flicking with his tongue.

Then his sweet savage assault turned once more to the heat between her thighs, searching for—and finding—the spot where his touch made her whimper in tender anguish.

Liz's legs parted in surrender, affording him the very core of her desire. His finger plunged inside her, and she met his penetrating rhythm with frenzied undulations.

Steve, delighted that she was every bit the warm, passionate woman he had dared to hope she would be, forced himself to draw away. "I have to get something…in the bedroom…come with me, please."

Liz took the hand he held out to her and followed him to the bed, where he laid her gently down before disappearing into the bathroom to sheath himself.

Then, positioning himself above her, she opened herself to him, lifting her legs to wrap about him as he settled between.

She clutched his back to pull him closer, but he was too lost in ecstasy to feel how her nails dug into his flesh. Then she was cupping his buttocks once more, this time squeezing and coaxing him to enter her all at once.

He was trying to be gentle, to make sure she could take the length of him, but with a deep, throaty cry, she tucked her heels against him to pull him forward.

He gave a mighty thrust, then gasped to feel the velvet of her close about him, soft, caressing, all the while urging him to take her wholly and completely.

He penetrated deeper, sculpting her tender woman flesh to receive him. Feeling the intensity of her own fever of desire inflamed him all the more, and his movements quickened.

Liz felt release coming...that overwhelming shudder from deep within her belly. Burrowing her face against his neck to stifle her cries of bliss, she made soft, whimpering sounds instead and clung tightly to him.

"Wonderful, oh, so wonderful," he cried in jubilation. Raining kisses over her face, he felt his own climax building. They would come together, to share in unison the fruition of the longing they had fought against for some time.

She rocked against him. The wake of her culmination washed into the crest of his own.

They clung together, breathing deep and hard, bodies sweat slicked and shuddering.

At last, like the ebb tide receding from a moon-kissed shore, the rapture settled about them in a quiet kind of bliss. Warm, satisfied, they continued to hold each other, reveling in every second of desire fulfilled.

Steve rolled to one side but held her against him, cradling her head on his shoulder as he stroked her hair and whispered, "I don't know what to say, sweetheart, except that I never knew it could be so good."

Serene moments passed, then Liz ventured to say lightly, "You don't know how glad I am to find out Mamie is actually a dog. I think I'm going to buy her a steak to celebrate."

Steve chuckled, "And I'll get Tom a big catfish all his own."

"Maybe we should take them on a picnic."

"How do you think it would work—the two of them together? Mamie is so gentle it might not be a problem with her, but how about Tom?"

Liz thought about it, then said, "Well, I think as long as she doesn't try to pull him out from under the bed when he's having quiet time, they might just make it."

Silence dropped once more as their gazes locked, held, each enraptured and assailed by the still-overwhelming reality of the wonder they had just experienced.

"I hope they do get along," Steve said, caressing her cheek with his fingertips, "because I hope we're going to be together for a long time, Liz."

"I...I'd like that," she stammered, heat rising once more at his touch. "I'd like it a lot, Steve. But let's make a promise here and now—no more lies. We have to be open and honest with each other if it's going to work."

"We will be," he assured.

"And I don't want it to be a problem for us working together."

"We won't let it. Nobody will notice anything. We'll be all business."

"Even on a stakeout?" she teased. "They get mighty boring, you know, and we might be tempted to find something to do to pass the time."

"No, we won't," he said with a sly grin. "We'll eat instead and get so fat we can't outrun a suspect."

"What are you talking about?" She could tell he was up to something.

He leaped out of bed, and she propped herself on her elbow to watch his luscious buns as he went to the dresser.

Opening a drawer, he pulled out a pair of pajama bottoms and quickly put them on, then threw the matching top to her. "Come on. Let's grab a quick shower, and I'll show you."

But the shower lasted longer than expected, because they caught fire again and wound up making love with water pouring down on them—a new, exhilarating experience for Liz and one she hoped to repeat often in the wonderful days that were surely ahead.

Finally they made it to the kitchen, which Liz was surprised to find spotless—as well as gourmet-equipped: convection oven, blender, food processor, grill-top range, big refrigerator and, she noted when he opened the door to the small pantry, very well stocked.

He took out the ingredients for a special omelet, which he proceeded to prepare in record time as Liz watched in awe.

When they were seated at the cozy table for two, attractively set like a display straight from Pier One, he waved at the food with a flourish and proudly declared, "This, my dear, is what I'm talking about. I'll just pack picnic lunches for our stakeouts, and when we get bored, we'll eat instead of making love."

Liz looked at the cheese and sausage omelet, framed by golden toast points and adorned with sliced kiwi fruit, then at the mugs of steaming espresso coffee from another gadget she hadn't noticed. There was also fresh-squeezed orange juice and a jar of strawberry jam.

She glanced from the food to him and gasped, laughed, and said, "I don't know what to say. You can cook."

"Yeah, it's a hobby of mine, but I don't have much time for it and usually call for takeout."

"I never would have thought," she murmured, amazed.

"Of course you didn't." He rolled his eyes. "And you dared call me sexist? Being a man doesn't rule out culinary talents, sweetheart."

She lifted her orange juice. "Oh, I will definitely drink to that."

They ate ravenously and talked and laughed about their mutual deceptions.

They talked, also, about the future and how they would, regardless of how hard it might be, manage to work together and not let their feelings for each other get in the way.

"We can't," Steve kept pointing out. "It's too dangerous. We have to focus on work. Nothing else."

"And no one can find out," Liz insisted, then teased, "so you'll have to keep on pretending you can't stand having me for your partner."

He fell sober. "It wasn't you, Liz. Like I told you, I have a thing about women in the dangerous end of police work. There are too many other areas to work in where it's safer. And don't tell me the story about the meter maid getting shot. I've heard it, and it was a freak accident."

She countered, "But there are dangers to any occupation…for both men and women."

"But not as a rule. I mean, you wear a gun, you have a custom-made bullet-proof vest, which means you're expected to be in life-threatening situations on a regular basis."

Liz ate the last bite of delicious omelet before reminding him, "I also happen to be trained for those life-threatening situations, you know."

He sighed. "Yeah, but I still don't like it, and I swore I'd never…" His voice trailed off. He had been about to divulge how he had sworn never again to get involved with a female partner but checked himself. At least he could keep that part of his vow—never to let anyone know how he blamed himself for Julie's death.

Liz lifted a brow. "Swore you would never what?"

"Never get involved with anybody I work with."

"What about that girl in California?"

His look told her she should not have gone there.

His soft laugh was forced and nervous. "What girl?"

"Oh, it was just something Carol Batson said." Liz shrugged, but wondered why he looked so upset if there was nothing to it. But they had promised never to lie to each other again, and she was not—absolutely not—going to allow doubt to creep into their relationship.

"And what was that?" he prodded.

She took a sip of coffee, which was wonderful, like everything else he had whipped together for their late-night snack. "Oh, she heard somewhere that you had left California because of a woman."

His laugh of incredulity, Liz noted, rang so false that she couldn't help pushing aside her resolve to never doubt him. "So is it true?"

"No," he shook his head firmly. "I left the West Coast because I wanted a change. That's all."

She offered a thin smile. "No ghosts in the past I need to know about?"

He abruptly rose and went to pull her up and into his arms. "You're the only woman in my life, Liz."

She hoped so.

Dear Lord, she hoped so.

Because somewhere along the way, despite all resolve and resolution, she had fallen helplessly, hopelessly, in love with Detective Steve Miller.

12

Liz awoke before Steve. She liked to do that...liked to have a few moments before the alarm went off to watch him sleeping. He had a little-boy look about him, hair mussed and falling across his forehead. Sometimes he would smile and mumble something indistinguishable, and she would wonder who he was dreaming about and hope it was her.

In the six weeks since that revelatory night when they each discovered the other was free of entanglements...free to explore whether their feelings for each other could grow into something truly meaningful and lasting, they had been together every moment possible.

Of course, everyone thought they went their separate ways when their work ended, but they would meet later, in out-of-the-way places for dinner or a movie. Sometimes they went bowling or in-line skating.

But the best part, Liz mused as she thrilled just to look at him, was when they could spend nights together. They alternated between her place and his. Steve liked to tease her about how she would have food delivered when they stayed at her apartment, but he had to slave in the kitchen when it was their turn there.

They teased each other in front of the other detectives, too, sometimes being sarcastic to the point of a near quarrel to thwart any suspicion that there might be a romance going on.

Liz brushed her lips across his forehead, intending to then slip out of bed and surprise him by making breakfast. But he surprised her by grabbing her and rolling her on top of him for a real kiss.

"You were awake all the time," she accused when he let her go, "watching me watching you."

"And how sweet it was, too," he grinned, giving her bottom a playful pat. "You do it all the time, too, don't you?"

"Well, maybe."

"Pervert," he teased.

"That's not being a pervert. Peeping Tom, maybe..."

"Speaking of Tom," he wagged a finger. "The next time that cat pounces on my feet when I get up in the night to go to the bathroom, he's toast."

She gave him a shove and rolled away. "You're crazy about that cat, and you know it."

"Well, he's not crazy about me." He pulled her close once more, wishing there was time now to make love to her, even though their passion of the night before had lasted till the wee hours.

Again she pulled away. Getting out of bed, she pulled a robe over her sleep T-shirt. "I was going to surprise you, but it's too late. Grab a shower while I make breakfast."

He covered his face with his hands and gave a mock groan. "Oh, no. She's going to cook. It's a conspiracy. She and the cat are both out to get me. I'm a goner...."

Snatching up a pillow, she pounded him with it. "That's mean, Steve Miller. I'm not that bad a cook, and you know it...."

He lunged for her wrist and jerked her to the bed, rolling on top of her and pinning her down. "What you are, my sweet, is a terrific lover, and I don't care if you can't boil water as long as we have this—''

He was about to kiss her, about to say to heck with food and getting to work on time, but just then their beepers went off at the same time.

They groaned in unison, and Liz said she would call in first, then he could respond after he got out of the shower. She headed for the living room, where she had left the remote phone.

Steve made no move to get out of bed. Instead, he allowed himself to become engulfed in guilt once more over the secret he yet harbored—and the lie he had told her. It seemed so easy to think about just saying, *Liz, I couldn't tell you before now, but the truth is I did leave California because of a woman. She was my partner, and I thought I was in love with her, but she got killed, and—*

And that was where it always ended—the obstacle he could not get around—that he blamed himself for Julie's death.

They'd had a fight that day. Nothing serious, but they were annoyed with each other. She accused him of flirting with a new female patrol officer. He had denied it, saying he was just being friendly. But Julie had been the jealous type and blew sky-high if he so much as glanced at another woman.

Usually he humbled himself and fawned all over her, promising she was the only woman for him and always would be, but he had begun to lose patience over what he felt was very immature behavior. So he had blown up right back at her and said he didn't give a damn whether she believed him or not.

Julie was not used to him reacting that way, and so they were hardly speaking when they answered the call that night. And when they arrived at the scene and he told her they should wait for backup, she had snapped that he couldn't tell her what to do, by damn, and off she'd gone—to her death.

He had known she was sensitive and high-strung, and if he had coddled her the way she'd needed, she would still be alive.

But how could he tell all that to Liz? She might say that if he'd known how Julie was, he should have forcefully stopped her that night, but then Liz would never feel secure around him again. Hell, he mused, frustrated, there was no telling what she would think. And she might even be mad enough to break up with him. After all, they had promised not to lie to each other, and she had asked him a direct question about a woman in California, and he had denied it.

Still, he wished he had the guts to come clean, because the truth was he loved her more every day and had started thinking that if she felt the same, they might wind up getting married. But then they would have to have a serious talk, because he didn't think he could ever get used to having his wife work as a detective. And she had already told him how her previous marriage had broken up because her ex didn't want her to be a cop.

Steve didn't know what to do, but knew something had to give soon, because he needed to focus on his work. It was too damn dangerous otherwise.

"A typical Monday morning, which means we've got to roll," Liz said, hurrying back into the bedroom. "That woman who was a witness in the grocery store robbery last week has finally shown up. Rogan says she's willing to talk now, and we've got to interrogate her before she loses her nerve. She's scared of retaliation, which means the robbers are probably from the neighborhood."

They showered together and dressed quickly—Steve in

suit, white shirt and tie; Liz in blazer, blouse, skirt and medium heels.

At the precinct, Steve automatically took over the interrogation of the eyewitness. He knew Liz really didn't enjoy doing it. In fact, he had started wondering just what she did like about being a detective. More and more, when they brought in a suspect, the first thing she did was run a make on him to find out whether he had a record. If she discovered he was on parole, she zeroed right in, trying to find out where things had gone wrong.

The witness cooperated. Steve got the information he needed to get a warrant on two suspects and told Liz he would have them drawn and proceed.

When they reached their office, however, Walt Rogan was standing outside with a big grin on his face. "You've got company, Miller."

He had no sooner made that announcement when a crowd of women led by Rosie Craddock rushed out the door holding balloons and cheering. Rosie carried a gaily wrapped package with a big bow on top.

They were celebrating the completion of the play area at Rosie's Trailer Park, as well as installation of the speed bumps. Their gift for him, purchased with contributions from every single resident, was a nice desk set.

They had brought a cake. Everyone in the bureau had a slice, and then the women left—after each gave him a big hug and kiss of appreciation.

When they were gone, Larry Spicer slapped Steve on the back and said, "You're their hero, Miller. I didn't know there were any left."

Mulvaney bantered, "What are you talking about, Spicer? He's the wind beneath their feet."

They were teasing, Liz knew, and meant no real harm, but she felt it wasn't right to make light of something so noble and immediately cut them down to size. "You clowns are just jealous, because you've never done anything that wonderful. And," she added reprovingly, "I seem to recall you didn't knock yourselves out with a financial donation to Steve's cause, but you sure pigged out on his cake."

They began to argue that they were just having a good time, but Liz waved them away. "I don't want to hear it. You're both insensitive clods, and you know it. So lay off Miller. He did something good...for a change," she added to keep from sounding too gushy with her praise.

"Thanks a lot, Casey," Steve said, feigning annoyance. "It's quite a treat to get a good word from you about anything."

"Hey, Casey," Rogan called from his office. "You've got a visitor downstairs. A woman by the name of Karen Booker."

"Who's that?" Steve asked Liz.

Liz brushed off his query. "Tell you later. Get those warrants so we can pick up the suspects as soon as I finish."

He called after her, but she kept on going, knowing he would have even more questions if she explained that Karen Booker was the wife of Alan Booker—the parolee who had held up the liquor store...and also held a gun to her head.

Karen, swollen in the last month of her pregnancy, was huddled on a bench in the busy lobby of the police station. Spotting Liz coming down the steps, she bolted up and ran to meet her. "Oh, thanks for seeing me, Detective Casey. I wasn't sure you'd have the time."

Liz accepted her hug, a bit self-conscious because others were watching with curiosity. It wasn't often officers received hugs in the lobby. Usually they were on the receiving end of curses and threats.

Leading her to a bench around a corner and out of sight, Liz asked, worried, "Is something wrong, Karen? Have you had bad news from Alan? I don't have any direct connection with the prison, but I try to keep up with how he's doing."

"I know you do, and I appreciate your phone calls to see how I'm getting along, too."

"So what brings you all the way down here?"

"I couldn't wait to tell you about what I found out when I saw him yesterday."

Liz knew Sunday was visiting day at Kilby prison, because she had been to see Alan a few times since he'd been sent back there. He had to complete his original sentence, plus six additional years for the liquor store robbery. "From the way you're smiling, it must be something good."

Karen Booker was glowing in her joy to share the news that her husband was being allowed to take computer classes. "And he's caught on so fast the warden says he can go to work in his office when he gets a little more experience. And you know what that could mean—with the warden giving him a break, he might be up for parole sooner. Oh, I know it'll be a couple of years. Alan did a bad thing trying to rob that store and everything else. But he's changed. I can tell he's changed. He's finally started believing in himself, after his parole officer had him thinking he was nothing but dirt. And we've got you to thank for it."

Liz was grateful for the words of praise but reminded her, "Alan had to want to change, Karen. And he had it in him to do it, too, which means that parole officer didn't know what he was talking about." The officer had been reprimanded, even though he'd denied the charges. Liz figured he would tread lightly with parolees in the future, which was all she could hope for.

Karen's eyes filled with happy tears, and she brushed them away with the back of her hand. "Well, you had the most to do with it. I think about all those times you visited him in jail when he was waiting for his trial, telling him how he could become a whole new person this time around, and I'm so grateful. And you were there at the trial, too, to let him know you cared. He's told me how much it meant, and we both owe you a lot."

"You don't owe me anything," Liz insisted. "Now what about you? What does the doctor say? How much longer before the baby is expected?"

Karen laughed and patted her huge tummy. "A couple more weeks. Ultrasound says it's a girl. We're going to name her after you."

Liz was touched, but again insisted she was owed no gratitude. Knowing Alan was on the way to rehabilitation was all she needed or wanted.

"You missed your calling," Karen said as she gave Liz a final hug in parting. "You should've been a parole officer instead of a cop. You'd do more good helping folks when they get out of jail instead of sending them there."

"Oh, I don't know about that, but thanks for all your kind words."

As Karen walked away, Liz thought of what she had said and realized, maybe for the first time, that she had enjoyed working with Alan Booker far more than anything else she had done in her career as a police officer.

"Hey, girlfriend."

She heard a familiar voice and turned to see Carol coming down the hall. "Well, what are you doing here?" Liz was further stunned to note she was wearing the uniform of the patrol division rather than traffic.

"Like it?" Carol twirled about, then patted her shoulder. "And did you notice this?"

It was the patch denoting First Precinct, and Liz's mouth fell open.

"Yep," Carol confirmed, "I am now a member of the patrol division of this precinct. And," she admonished, "if you hadn't been ignoring your friends these past weeks, you'd have known that. I've called, left messages—"

"I know, I know, and I'm sorry." Liz was washed with guilt to think how she had been so busy with Steve—as well as trying to keep their relationship secret—that she had been out of personal touch with lots of people. Even her family was complaining about how she had not visited lately. "So tell me what brought all this about," she urged, anxious to turn attention from herself.

Carol explained that she had finally decided she needed to do something with her life besides wait for Mister Right to come along and decided to devote more time to her career. She was taking night classes and had demonstrated her willingness to advance, and when the opening in patrol had come along in First Precinct, she had applied for it and been accepted.

"So here I am," she said proudly. "We'll be seeing more of each other this way.

"But now it's your turn," she said, eyes narrowing as she got serious. "What's going on that keeps you so busy in your off hours? Who's the guy?"

"Uh, nobody," Liz hedged, then thought of Karen Booker and proceeded to explain about how she had taken an interest in Alan Booker and spent time visiting him, as well as his family.

Carol was impressed. "Wow. That's really something. Maybe you should've been a parole officer."

Liz laughed. "You're the second person who's told me that this morning."

"So? Why couldn't you be one if you wanted to? With your background in law enforcement, you shouldn't have a bit of trouble."

"Oh, I'd need to take special courses."

"Which you could do."

"Which would give my dad a heart attack," Liz said, frowning as she thought of how he would react to the idea. "He's so proud of me for being a detective, but he's always felt parole officers had sissy jobs."

Carol reminded, "It's your life, honey."

"I know, but I've never thought about being anything besides a cop. I even thought Pop might not want me to be a detective and insist I really stick to tradition and just be on the beat or in patrol."

"Maybe it's time you started thinking for yourself. You aren't getting any younger, you know. And if you want to make a change, now is the time to do it. But say—" she rushed to another topic "—how's 'the hunk'? Are you two still teamed up together? I haven't heard. Nobody sees him at the Blue Spot anymore."

Liz suddenly felt uncomfortable. Carol was very astute and picked up on things quickly, so she didn't want to dwell on the subject of Steve. "Yeah, sure. We get on real well. Now tell me more about your new job."

"You know about my new job," Carol said quietly, evenly. "It used to be yours, remember? What I want to know is why you're always so reluctant to talk about Steve Miller."

Liz knew how a suspect must feel beneath Steve's relentless grilling. "Because there's nothing to talk about. He's my partner. We work together. That's it."

"He's also gorgeous. Like I've told you before, every

single female cop I know would give her last pair of run-free panty hose for a date with him. Me included. You're with him all the time. You're single. You've got to feel the same way, unless he's really a creep.''

''Oh, he's not a creep. Quite the contrary.'' She told her about how he had raised funds for the playground at Rosie's Trailer Park, the speed bumps and also the party just that morning in his honor. ''Underneath the toughness, he's got a tender side, which is great. Other than that—'' Liz forced a careless smile and threw up her hands ''—what can I tell you? He's my partner, but that's it. He doesn't turn me on.'' She almost grabbed her nose to see if it had gotten any bigger with such a whopper of a lie.

Carol bit her lip thoughtfully. ''So he's standoffish, huh? Never made a pass? Never hinted he might be interested in you?''

''That's right.''

''And you're about the best-looking single gal around,'' Carol continued to muse aloud. ''You know what I think?''

Liz shook her head. ''Nope, and I don't have time to hear it, either. I've really got to run, Carol. Let's do lunch first chance, okay?'' She turned away.

''I think it's the woman in California.''

Liz swung back around, tension creeping. There it was again—the rumor about Steve having left his job in L.A. because of a broken heart. But he had denied it, and after they had made a pact never to be anything but totally honest with each other, Liz didn't want to hear anything to make her think he wasn't keeping his part of that agreement. ''What woman?'' she asked edgily.

''I told you—I don't know all the details,'' Carol explained. ''Just that him leaving to come here had to do with a woman. The way I figure, she dumped him for another guy, and he couldn't stand the humiliation, so he left town.'' She swung her head from side to side in wonder. ''Jeez, can you imagine any woman being stupid enough to dump a hunk like Miller?''

''No, no, I can't,'' Liz said thinly, knowing she had to end the conversation then and there or she might give herself away. ''Look. I've really got to go. He's waiting on me. We've got warrants to pick up two suspects, and we're afraid they'll skip if we don't get on it right away.''

''All right. But you've got to promise to save some time for me. It's been too long since we had a fun night out together.''

''Sure, I'll call you.''

They were about to go in opposite directions, but just then Carl Bundy leaned over his dispatcher's desk to yell to Liz, ''Hey, Casey. Tell Miller some woman wants to see him. Says it's important.''

Hearing that, Carol, always curious, hung back to see what was going on.

Liz, figuring it could only be business, called back to Bundy, ''Tell her it will have to wait awhile. We're on our way to make a bust.''

Suddenly a woman came around the desk, high heels clicking against the tile floor as she rushed toward Liz. She was stylishly dressed in a suit with a fitted jacket and short skirt that showed off her curvaceous figure. She had blond hair that flowed down her back like liquid silver, and her makeup looked as if it had been done by a professional.

''Please, wait.'' She held out long slim fingers capped by perfect acrylic nails. ''I have to see Steve. He's an old friend, and I don't have a lot of time.''

Liz couldn't help feeling a twinge of apprehension, and, yes, jealousy, too. ''Well, I can tell him you're here,'' she said hesitantly, ''but like I said, we're on our way out. He'll probably say you'll have to wait.''

Her laugh was like little silver bells tinkling in a summer breeze, and, sounding very sure of herself, said, "Oh, when he finds out it's me, he'll take a moment."

Carol blurted, "Are you from California?"

The woman saw her for the first time and swept her with a gaze that said she found her nosy. "Why, yes, I am. So you know Steve, too?"

Carol lifted her chin. "Not as well as Detective Casey, here. She's his partner."

Gold-tipped lashes dusted creamy cheeks as the woman blinked and turned to Liz once more. "Would you please tell him that Marla Nivens is here? We've known each other a long time, but when he left Los Angeles, I lost track of him. It's taken me a while to locate him."

"Maybe he didn't want you to find him," Carol said impulsively, and Liz jabbed her with an elbow.

Marla's eyes flashed with contempt as she snapped, "Steve had some problems he had to work out. I would have heard from him sooner or later. But I finally persuaded someone in L.A. records to tell me where he'd gone, and—"

"And I'll tell him you're here," Liz said, turning toward the stairs. The way the woman was prattling on, she might wind up telling what had caused the breakup between her and Steve, and Liz didn't want to hear it. She was having a hard enough time grasping the fact that he had lied, without having to endure intimate details, as well.

"Hey, Liz, call me later," Carol yelled after her.

Liz knew it wouldn't be necessary. Carol would probably be camped on her doorstep when she got home, waiting to hear the whole story.

But she won't get it from me, Liz thought, anger boiling through her veins as she walked toward the office, chin up, jaw set, because she wouldn't listen to anything Steve had to say. She couldn't trust him to tell the truth, anyway.

He was waiting at her desk, holding the envelope with the warrants in his hand and looking quite perturbed. "What kept you so long, Casey? I've asked Mulvaney and Spicer to go with us, because I just found out—" He saw the flashing rage in her eyes, the tight set of her lips, and quickly asked, "What's wrong?"

Aware that others were around and could hear, Liz made herself sound pleasant as she told him, "You have a visitor downstairs."

"You're kidding." He laughed—but uneasily, because she looked mad enough to bite a nail in half. "I don't have time. We've got to roll on this before those two find out the witness talked and take off. Now we know where they are, and—"

Liz cut him off. "She says you'll want to see her and to tell you her name is Marla Nivens."

Liz watched, her heart cracking like a dam under pressure from rising flood waters, as Steve paled. His eyes went wide. His mouth gaped open, and then he began to move his lips wordlessly.

She saw, too, how the warrants he held in his hand went fluttering to the floor.

Without a word, he brushed by her and all but ran from the office.

Mulvaney and Spicer, who had just walked up, looked from Steve to the warrants he had dropped, and Spicer asked, "What's with him?"

"Never mind," Liz said, bending to retrieve the papers. "He's probably going to be gone for a while. Hell, he might not even come back. Let's roll."

The two men exchanged incredulous looks, then rushed to keep up with her as she headed out.

13

Steve's heart was pounding almost as loud as his feet as he hurried downstairs.

"It's nice to see you again, Steve," Marla said quietly when he reached her. "It took me a long time to find you, and there were times when I was afraid I wasn't going to."

He led her across the hall to the lounge, which he was grateful to find empty. He waited till he closed the door after them before taking a deep breath and asking, "So exactly how did you find me?"

She walked over to one of the many sofas crowded into the room and sat down.

There was a table nearby with a pot of hot coffee and a plate of doughnuts, but Steve wasn't concerned with being polite and offered neither. He tried to read her expression and saw only that she didn't appear to be angry.

She tugged absently at one of her earrings, and he wondered why she seemed so nervous. He was the one who was feeling wound up tight enough to break. After all, the last time he had seen Marla's sister had been at the funeral, when she had told him afterward in no uncertain terms that she, and the rest of the family, held him responsible for Julie's death.

Finally, as though having mustered the courage, Marla cleared her throat and began. "It wasn't easy. None of your friends knew where you'd gone, and if they did, they wouldn't tell me.''

"They didn't know. No one did.''

"Except for personnel. I figured out you'd have to go back to work sooner or later, and they would have a record of where your references were sent.''

He frowned. "They promised me that that would all be kept confidential. I wanted to make a new life without having to worry about somebody from the past reminding me of nightmares I'd like to forget.... Like now,'' he added grimly, pointedly.

He hadn't sat down, leaning instead against the door, arms folded across his chest.

Marla squirmed beneath his angry gaze. "Don't be mad at me for coming here, Steve. Hear me out, please.''

"I'm waiting, but you still haven't told me how you found me—how you got personnel to give you restricted information.''

"Everyone has a price. And so did one of the girls in personnel. It cost me five hundred dollars, but it will be well worth it, along with my plane ticket, if I can make things right with you.''

He felt the hurricane in his gut speed up to a "category five.'' He had never cared for Marla. Though beautiful, she was spoiled and self-centered...and very fortunate that Nick Nivens, her husband, put up with her. He was a hardworking building contractor, and though he wasn't rich by California standards, he managed to make it possible for Marla to shop Rodeo Drive now and then to keep her happy.

He spoke coldly and evenly. "The last time I saw you, Marla, you were screaming at me that I had killed your baby sister by upsetting her so she didn't know what she was doing. You used a lot of four-letter words and called me street names I'd never have guessed you knew. You were one of the reasons I wanted to 'get out of Dodge.' So why in hell are you here now, wasting my time by not making any sense?''

''Because I realized later I had no right to say those things to you. I was stricken with grief and wanting to lash out at somebody, so it was easy to blame you. I felt terrible afterward, and I've been trying to find you ever since. You weren't responsible for Julie's death.''

''How can you be so sure?'' he cocked a brow. ''I mean, you don't know anything that went on that night between us, Marla. You had nothing on which to base your accusation, just like you have no justification now for retracting it.''

She looked ready to cry. ''Oh, yes, I do, Steve, because I knew the real Julie. You didn't. She was willful and headstrong, and no one could tell her anything. When she joined the police force, the whole family worried that she'd wind up in trouble, because she just wasn't the type to take orders.''

Steve wished she would get to the point. He needed to get back to Liz and try to straighten things out with her. Hell, she probably thought Marla was the woman in California she had asked him about…and who he had also lied about to keep from telling her what had happened.

''I was aware of that,'' he snapped impatiently. ''We were working on it. But the truth was—she was mad at me that night and wouldn't listen when I told her to wait for backup. Any other time she would have, but right before that I'd gotten tired of always being the one to give in when we had a fight, and I let her know it. My mistake was in picking the wrong time to do it. So it was my fault, and I'm afraid you wasted your time coming here to try and make me believe otherwise—though it was nice of you to do it.''

Marla shook her head. ''You're wrong. The fight you'd had earlier didn't have anything to do with that night.''

He straightened. ''What do you mean?''

''She called me from work that afternoon and told me about it, claiming you'd been flirting with somebody. I told her she was being silly, that you were an all-right guy and she was lucky to have you.''

Steve gratefully recalled that at one time Marla had been an ally, taking his part when he and Julie had problems.

She continued, ''That made her mad at me. She said I didn't know what I was talking about, that you were only out for yourself, ready to walk over anybody that might get in your way to keep you from making lieutenant.''

Steve remembered how he had been bucking for promotion back then, but he hadn't given it a thought since. ''She said that? But—''

''I know, I know,'' Marla's head bobbed up and down in her eagerness to tell him everything. ''You weren't like that, but I'm afraid Julie couldn't stand being out-bested any more than she could stomach taking orders. She told me *she* would get that promotion—not you, that she was through doing what you told her just to make you look good. She was going to get some attention, some praise.

''Oh, don't you see, Steve?'' Marla bounded to her feet. ''Her not waiting for backup had nothing to do with being mad at you over the fight you'd had. She had already made up her mind she was going to do whatever it took to win a citation…to look good so she could get the promotion instead of you. That's why she was reckless that night. I doubt you could have saved her if you'd tried, unless you were willing to physically hold her back.''

"Which I should have done," he said between clenched teeth.

"Be that as it may," she acceded, "you cannot blame yourself for what she did. You had no way of knowing she was scheming to outdo you."

Hurt rolled in his stomach, and he wished somehow he had never found out the truth, even if it meant continuing to bear the guilt of what had happened that night. Sometimes it was best to let secrets be buried, but Marla had done what she felt was right. She had also acted to make herself feel better about herself, but he could forgive her that.

She retrieved her purse from the sofa where she had dropped it. "I can't begin to tell you how awful I felt when I heard you'd quit the force and left town. I realized then it probably had to do with the terrible things I said to you, and I made up my mind I'd move heaven and earth to find you and set the record straight."

She started toward the door, but paused. "I want you to know something else, too, Steve. It wasn't easy for me to tell you all this. I loved Julie, and I feel I've betrayed her."

"Thank you for coming, Marla." He started to shake her hand but hugged her instead.

They clung together for a moment, and then she broke away and ran out of the room.

He knew she was crying and made up his mind he would call her later and thank her again. He would also stay in touch, because it was suddenly important that she not be the one to harbor guilt, for he well knew the agony of doing so.

Returning to the office, he found it empty and hurried to Rogan. "Where is she—where's Casey?"

Rogan looked up from his paperwork with a puzzled

expression. "What do you mean? She's gone to serve the warrants."

"By herself?" Steve yelped.

"No. Mulvaney and Spicer went with her."

He slammed his fist on Rogan's desk. "I wanted to scope things out first. We might need to call in SWAT if those guys decide to make a stand. We know they've got firearms. Hell, according to reports, one of them was carrying an Uzi."

Leaning back in his chair, Rogan was quiet for a moment, then said, "I think you'd better get a grip, Miller. Casey is a good officer, and she's got two good men with her. Among the three of them, I think they can figure out how to handle whatever comes up."

Steve could see the wheels turning inside the chief's head as he wondered what was going on, why he was so upset. So he forced himself to calm down quickly. "You're right. I just don't like being left behind. I'll get on over there."

He had to take the time to go back to the files and locate the copy of the warrants in order to get the address, because he couldn't remember it. All he knew was that it was in a tenement section—big, sprawling and rundown.

It was a hell of a place for a shootout, he groused as he sped toward the scene in his personal car. The only department vehicles available were marked cruisers, and he wasn't about to use any of them. It was necessary to ease into the area unnoticed, get in position, then think how best to handle it. Still, he wished for a flashing blue light to use while he struggled to get through lunch hour traffic in downtown Birmingham.

When he arrived at last, he spotted Mulvaney and Spicer's car parked at the very edge of the complex. They were nowhere to be seen. He decided to take a quick drive around and locate the apartment, which Liz would have done so she would know which way to head after leaving her car. It was no time to ask other occupants for directions. They might be in cahoots with the suspects and warn them someone was asking about them.

It took him five minutes to find the location, and he wondered why Mulvaney and Spicer had parked so far away and where the hell they had gone, because he didn't spot them anywhere. Then he decided they must have gotten out of their car and gone in Liz's, so he circled around again to search for it.

At last he saw it—parked behind a row of Dumpsters way in the back. Again he was frustrated as to why it was so far from the apartment where the suspects were thought to be. Maybe Liz and the guys had decided to be extra cautious. The place seemed deserted, few cars around. No kids playing in the streets, which was good. So even though it was a bonus not to have civilians around in case shooting broke out, the lack of traffic also made it easier to spot unfamiliar vehicles which could raise a warning flag.

Leaving his car, he cut behind the buildings on foot, hoping all the while that Liz wouldn't approach the front door of that apartment building. She was wearing her usual clothes and not a bullet-proof vest, because by the time he'd decided they needed to suit up and call out SWAT—after he'd run a check and found out the two suspects had rap sheets longer than his arm—Marla had shown up and he'd lost it. He'd left without telling Liz and the other team how bad the situation was.

He supposed he could be forgiven for having momentarily spun out of control. After all, it had been like hearing a voice from the grave to have Marla show up. Still, he wished he had reacted differently. Given the circumstances at the time, however, he figured his shock was understandable. He only hoped he could make Liz understand everything...if he could even get her to listen.

Steve had found the suspects' address by checking city utility listings on computer. Then a quick call to the Credit Bureau divulged both of them were working at a fast-food restaurant. One more discreet, carefully-worded inquiry and he had learned neither had been seen for several days. So they were either holed up together in the apartment, waiting for the excitement over the robbery to calm down, or had already blown town.

He spotted a square building with a sign that said "Laundromat" on a corner almost directly across from the apartment. Another hunch struck—that Liz and the guys might be using it for their surveillance point.

He was right.

He stepped through the door and found all three crouched beneath a window.

"Get in here and get down," Larry Spicer gruffly whispered. "They're in there, all right. We just saw them go in maybe ten minutes ago. We're getting ready to make our move."

"Not without SWAT, you aren't. I didn't have a chance to tell you before, but I've got a make on those two, and they're dangerous. It would be suicide to walk up and knock on their door." Steve whipped his cell phone from his pocket. He didn't look at Liz but could feel her eyes on him, rage sizzling like a barbecue grill on the Fourth of July. He prayed it would all be over soon so he could get her off by herself and try to square things, because he had realized he loved her beyond belief and couldn't bear the thought of losing her. And, oh, how he wished he'd been honest from the get-go. But he would make it up to her, by God, and—

"I say we get out of here," Liz surprised everybody by suddenly, sharply, proclaiming.

Steve was punching numbers and looked up to ask her why.

"Because somebody might come in here. We're lucky it was empty, but if somebody decides to wash clothes, we're going to have to run them out, and we don't know any of these people. The suspects might have a lot of friends around."

Steve noted she not only looked mad, she sounded mad—really mad—but Spicer and Mulvaney were too intent on the situation to pick up on any vibes at the moment. Later they might wonder, but he didn't care about that— didn't care about anything but neutralizing the present mess they were in and retreating to a safe point to wait for the cavalry to arrive.

"I'll go along with that," Spicer said.

Mulvaney agreed, "Me, too."

Steve held up his hand as his call answered. Firing words like bullets he gave the order for the SWAT team to come running, then disconnected. "Okay," he said. "You might have been lucky to have gotten this far without being seen, but let's move slow from here on out. We can't walk out together."

"We've got to walk out fast, though," Spicer said, stealing a look out the window. "Two women are coming this way with laundry baskets."

"Worse news," Mulvaney informed them as he focused binoculars on the apartment windows. "I see movement near the front door. They might be coming out again."

Steve began to sweat. "Casey, you're out of here first," he brusquely ordered, motioning her toward the door. "Walk out at a normal pace and look like you know where you're going. Don't glance around."

She looked at the three of them in turn. "What about the rest of you?"

"I'm staying here to keep an eye on things. I'll make like I'm waiting for a load of clothes to wash."

He dug in his pocket for three quarters, stuffed them in the slot of the nearest machine to start it, then took off his coat and tossed it aside in an effort to look casual. "Now go, damn it," he tersely ordered her. "The guys will go around the corner and take the long way back to the Dumpster. I don't want it to appear you're all together."

Her anger with him dissipated as she asked with a stricken look on her face, "Are you going to be okay?" Despite everything, Liz knew she loved him, and even if he and Marla Nivens had smoothed things over and were back together, she still cared what happened to him...and always would.

"I'll be fine. Now, please, go...."

Spicer and Mulvaney were already on their way. They knew the approaching women would be alarmed to find them there and might start screaming.

Liz hung back. "You don't look much like a wash woman," she said, attempting to lighten the tense moment. But before he could lambaste her for not moving fast enough, she stepped out the door.

Steve rushed to peer out the window and cursed to see two men had come out of the apartment. They had started toward a car, parked at the curb, but slowed to stare first at Mulvaney and Spicer as they disappeared around the corner, then Liz.

"Don't look back, Liz," Steve urged under his breath as he watched her. "Keep on going, baby. Don't look toward them no matter what you do."

But Liz didn't know they had come outside, didn't know that they had seen her and were wondering what she was doing coming out of the laundromat, dressed as she was. Neither was she aware of how they were also puzzled as to why two men in business suits had appeared just before she did.

So she turned to take one last look, to ensure the area was still secure. It seemed instinctive to do so.

Steve groaned, "Oh, God, baby, no..."

"Cops," one of the men roared. He started back inside.

Liz heard and instinctively went for her gun, but one of the suspects had already drawn his.

Steve lunged for the door shouting, "Liz, get down—"

The man fired at Steve, and with a pain ripping into his back like a bolt of liquid fire, Steve crumpled to his knees, then slumped to the sidewalk.

Liz fired off one round toward the gunman, but he had already made it back inside. "Oh, no, please, God, no," she wailed, running for Steve.

Spicer and Mulvaney had heard the shot and raced back from the opposite side of the Laundromat.

His gun in hand, Spicer kept a bead on the apartment to cover as Mulvaney helped Liz drag Steve back inside the laundromat.

Gently they maneuvered him onto his back. "Call for an ambulance," she barked the order. "Tell them we've got an officer down."

Mulvaney did so on his cell phone, then dropped beside her. "How bad is it?"

"I—I'm not sure." She willed her hands to stop trembling so she could begin CPR, because his breathing was shallow, and she knew he needed all the help he could get. "He was hit in the back. He's bleeding bad. I've got to be careful...not make it worse...." She was talking to herself, not Mulvaney, trying to get a grip and do what had to be done in an effort to save Steve's life. But dear God, she had never felt so helpless in her life.

Mulvaney left her to join Spicer in his vigil at the window. "I hope the bastards make a break for it," he told him, face twisted with anger. "I'll blow 'em to hell, so help me."

"Steve, can you hear me?" Liz bent to check his breathing, but it was even more faint. She gave up pumping his chest, fearing it would hurt him even worse to press on him when she didn't know where the bullet was. Already she could hear a siren in the distance. The experts would soon arrive to take over.

She stretched beside him to lift his head in her arms and cradle him against her. "Please, please hear me," she whispered.

His eyes were closed. He lay very still.

"Please, honey, just hang on. Help is on the way. You've got to make it...." Her tears splashed upon his face, and she kissed them away as she avowed, "I love you, and I always will."

From far, far away, Steve thought he heard a voice—Liz's voice. Was she near? he wondered. Because he was drifting away and had to tell her, had to make her understand about—

"Marla..."

At first, Liz dared to hope it had only been a moan of pain, anguish, that he hadn't really spoken the name.

"Marla..."

He said it again, and she knew it was no mistake.

His head slumped to one side.

She continued to hold him as she wept, her lips pressed against his ear as she told him over and over that she loved him...and tried not to think how he had called another woman's name with what might have been his last breath.

14

"**I** think you're crazy," Carol said, pushing away the pizza Liz had ordered for them. Since joining the patrol division she paid more attention to physical fitness and watched her diet closely.

Liz was surprised to see her pass up her favorite junk food—especially when it was loaded with pepperoni. She reached for a slice, then changed her mind. She was determined not to try and fill the cracks of her broken heart with saturated fat.

Carol sighed, exasperated. "Aren't you going to say anything? I came all the way over here to tell you Steve is going to make it and also that he's asking to see you, and all you do is sit there like a knot on a log. He's your partner, for crying out loud."

"Not any more he isn't."

Carol's mouth fell open. "Since when? What happened? I thought you said you two were getting along great these days. And from what I heard, he took the bullet meant for you, which means he saved your life, and you aren't grateful? You won't even go see him his first day out of intensive care? What is wrong with you, girlfriend?" Her eyes narrowed. "I know—it's that Barbie doll from California, right? She's the one who dumped him, and she snapped her fingers, and now he's going to go running back to her."

"I...I wouldn't know about that," Liz said chokingly. All she knew was that Steve had called Marla Nivens's name with what might well have been his dying breath, had the paramedics not arrived to save him. Whether or not he went back to her was beside the point. She was the one he was thinking about in his darkest hour, and that pretty well frosted the cake, as far as Liz was concerned.

"Then what? What reason could you have for refusing to see him?"

"It's personal."

"Aha." Carol slapped her hands together. "That's it. You two did have something going between you, didn't you? I knew it. I could tell. All the signs were there—how you seemed to drop out of sight when you were off duty, never answering your phone or returning calls. You were with him, and you fell for him, and Barbie showed up and that was it."

"Carol, I really don't want to talk about this."

But Carol wasn't listening, because something had just dawned. "Wait a minute. If that were so, she would've been there, wouldn't she? Hanging around ICU. But the only visitors he's had were detectives. I know, because I heard somebody say how sad it was he didn't have any family. So that means Barbie wasn't there."

"Her name is Marla, Carol. Not Barbie." Liz wished she hadn't felt the need to invite her over, but she was, after all, a friend. Besides, she thought guiltily, she needed a favor, so she got to the point of why she wanted to see her. "Look, I need your help. I'm moving out of my apartment and can't find a place to stay right away. I want to bunk with you if it's okay. I'll do my share, help pay the rent and all."

Carol was even more bewildered. "Well, sure, but what's going on?"

"I'm quitting the force."

Carol gasped. "You're kidding. I don't believe it. Oh, jeez, Liz, what happened between you and Miller to make you do a thing like that?"

Liz wished she could tell her everything, because she truly needed to unload. It might make her feel better, because it was rough keeping so much grief locked inside. But quitting the force, she had decided after careful consideration, was her first step to leaving the pain behind. "I've decided I want to be a parole officer."

"Are you serious?"

"Very serious. After working with Alan Booker, I realized that's what I want to do—help parolees make a new start. I don't think anything I've ever done has made me feel so good about myself. Did you know they're going to name their daughter after me?" she asked, smiling. "But I've got to take a couple of courses at the technical college before I can be a full-fledged parole officer. You live pretty close to the college, so that will be convenient. And I've already talked to the Bessemer parole office. They've agreed to let me work part-time as an assistant till I get certified."

Carol was quick to ask, "And what about your dad? Have you told him?"

She nodded. It hadn't been as bad as she'd thought it would be, but that probably had to do with the fact he was so relieved she hadn't been shot. There had been a big story in the paper when it had happened nearly three weeks earlier. The SWAT team had arrived to quickly force the suspects out with tear gas, and no one else was hurt. Steve would eventually receive a citation for having defended a fellow officer by risking his own life. Hearing all that, her father had second thoughts about the danger of the profession when it was his daughter that had almost gotten killed.

"He's accepted it. He says if that's what I want to do, fine. He'd never really considered that being a parole officer was part of the police force, so he's got to come to terms with that and how the family tradition won't be carried on. But he'll eventually get used to the idea. My mother is over the moon about it, she's so happy."

Carol appeared unwilling to let go of her suspicions about a romance between Liz and Steve and continued to try to pry it out of her. "All this really has to do with Miller, though, doesn't it? I mean, him going back to his old girlfriend really hit you between the eyes, and now you can't bear to be around him."

Tom ambled into the room, meowing for attention. Seeing him made Liz recall that wonderful night when the desire she and Steve had been fighting against for so long came to light. They'd experienced precious hours of sweet lovemaking, whispered promises...and whispered lies.

She hadn't realized she was crying until Carol said, "See? I'm right. You are in love with him. Now let's hear it. I want the whole story, or you can find another place to crash."

Liz doubted she would refuse to let her move in with her, but decided her tears had given her away, anyway. "Yes, I am in love with him, Carol, but he doesn't love me. He loves Marla."

"I thought so," Carol declared with satisfaction. "But weren't you worried that would happen—that they'd eventually get back together if he was so torn over them breaking up that he came all the way here to try and get over her?"

"No, because I asked him about her after you told me what you'd heard. He denied it."

Carol slapped her knees. "The lying creep. But I still

think you ought to fight for him. I mean, if he's asking for you—''

"But it wasn't me he was asking for when he thought he was dying.''

"You mean he called Barbie's name?''

"Marla,'' Liz corrected again. "He called Marla's name.''

"Whatever,'' Carol said with a shrug and a sneer. "Well, I don't blame you for not going to see him. It's a matter of pride. And I don't blame you for leaving the force, either. I wouldn't want to be around him for fear I'd give him a swift kick you-know-where.''

"He'll probably go back to California to be with her.''

Carol reminded her, "But we still haven't figured out why she hasn't been around while he was listed in critical condition.''

"Well, it doesn't matter. I've got to put him out of my mind.''

"Do that later,'' Carol said. "I want to hear some more about all this.''

"There's nothing to tell.''

"Yes, there is. What did he do when he caught up with you at the apartment complex before the shooting started? Did he apologize or act guilty or anything?''

"There wasn't time to even notice. I know I was mad and trying not to let it show, but things happened real fast.'' Liz took one of the paper napkins that had been delivered with the pizza and folded it to dab at her eyes. "But the fact remains he still saved my life, and I'm grateful, but I don't even want to be around him long enough to tell him that. I just want to walk away from it, Carol, walk away and make a new life for myself and not look back.''

Carol reached to pat her shoulder. "Well, if that's the

way you want to handle it, I'll help all I can. Now when do you want to start packing?"

Liz had also carefully planned her move. "Right away. My rent isn't up till the first of the month, but I want to go ahead and get out of here. I'm afraid Steve will be on a guilt trip and try to find me to soothe his conscience—if he even has one—by attempting to apologize, and I don't want to hear any more of his lies. So I'm not leaving any forwarding address, and Chief Rogan has assured me my personnel file will be sealed so nobody can find out where I've gone."

Carol's eyes bugged. "What did you tell him to get him to agree to do that? Did you have to admit you and Steve were involved?"

"No. And he didn't ask for an explanation. I think he figures the shooting was pretty traumatic for me, and my way of dealing with it is to resign from being a detective and leave the force. He's not about to argue with that. Besides, I let him know my decision was carved in stone."

Carol was thoughtful for a moment, then looked Liz straight in the eye. "I just want to know one thing—are you one hundred percent certain this is what you want? You could still go to the hospital to see him, you know, find out what he's got to say, and while you're there tell him to go to hell." Her eyes were glittering.

"Yes, I am certain this is what I want," Liz assured, leaning to lift Tom to cradle in her arms. She pressed her cheek against his soft fur and blinked back more tears. "And it doesn't matter what he wants to say to me. I just have to get busy trying to get over him, but I do love him, and I told him so when I was holding him in my arms that day. I'd never said so before. We didn't talk about love. We just enjoyed being together. But I thought he was dying, and I wanted him to know. And that's when he called

Marla's name," she said brokenly, "right after I told him
I loved him."

Steve was propped against the pillows of his hospital
bed. His supper tray of chicken noodle soup and Jell-O was
untouched.

"You aren't going to get your strength back by not eating," Mulvaney warned. He was sitting next to the bed,
having brought some magazines his wife thought Steve
might enjoy reading. "They'll be sticking that IV needle
back in if you don't watch out."

Steve couldn't help it. He hadn't yet regained his appetite. The bullet had been removed—along with his spleen,
but the doctors assured him he would be fine without it.
He had also been told that in a month or so he could go
back on active duty. So he was lucky and grateful to be
alive, and the only thing keeping him from feeling one
hundred percent okay was not having heard from Liz.

"How's Casey doing?" he asked Mulvaney, calling her
by her last name to keep from sounding intimate. All officers called each other by last names. It's just how it was.

Mulvaney zeroed in on a picture hanging on a far wall
to keep from looking at Steve. "Okay, I guess."

Steve tried to sit up straighter, but he was still sore from
the incision across his upper left side and couldn't quite
make it. "What do you mean—*you guess?* She's working,
isn't she? It's been three weeks. I can understand if she
took off a few days. She's bound to have been upset by
everything that happened, but she should be back by now.
She's a strong woman."

"Yeah, yeah, she is, and she came back."

"Then how is she doing? I've been wondering why she
hasn't been to see me," he added, hating to sound so concerned, but damn it, he was. He had tried calling her re-

peatedly in the one day he had been out of intensive care and had a phone beside his bed, but there was no answer and her machine wasn't turned on. He had even tried her beeper, but she hadn't responded.

Mulvaney gestured to the magazines on the bedside table. "Do you see anything in there you want to read? If not, I can get some more. Just give me a list—"

"I don't care about reading, Mulvaney," Steve snapped impatiently. "I just want to know about Casey. It's funny she hasn't been around."

Mulvaney focused on the picture again. "Well, you'll have to ask her. I wouldn't know anything about that."

"I have tried to ask her. I've been trying all day, but I can't get hold of her. Now, when did you last see her? What has she said about me? It's just damn weird that my own partner can't take a minute to come check on me, especially when I took her bullet." He hated to throw that up, and never would to Liz, but he was frustrated, and it just popped out.

Mulvaney confided, "The truth is, the last time I saw her was the week after it happened—when she showed up to clean out her desk and locker."

Again Steve tried to sit up, as though by doing so he could grasp the situation and deal with it. The pain was intense, but he fought against it and succeeded. "You mean she's gone? She transferred to another department?"

"I don't know. Nobody does except Rogan, and he's not saying. Us guys figure she went home—to Montgomery— maybe to work with her dad. Or maybe she's giving up police work. Who knows? Something like what happened that day can affect a person in strange ways. I mean, like you said, you took her bullet and almost died doing it. That's bound to give her second thoughts. Some people can handle it. Some can't.

"Well," he slapped his knees and stood up. "I gotta go. I dropped the wife at the mall, and I've got to pick her up because it's nearly closing time. Anything I can do for you?"

Steve gingerly lowered himself back to the pillows. "No...nothing."

"Call me if there is."

"Yeah, thanks."

The door closed after Mulvaney, and Steve gritted his teeth and stared up at the ceiling.

Why, he wondered with heavy heart, would Liz have done such a thing? Surely if she had cared anything at all about him, she would have given him a chance to explain everything...especially when he had almost died for her.

But maybe, he rationalized, she really didn't care, and that was why she'd left. She felt guilty over what he'd done, when he'd actually meant nothing to her.

He told himself he must have only thought he heard her telling him how much she loved him after he'd been shot. Wishful thinking, maybe, in the dizzy, fading moments, as he drifted in and out of consciousness.

She couldn't have said the words and leave so abruptly, but then how could he know the depth of hurt and rage she'd felt over discovering he'd lied about his past? Who did she really think Marla was? There hadn't been a chance to tell her.

The door opened and a nurse breezed in, took one look at his supper tray, and immediately scolded him. "Mr. Miller, if you don't eat, I'm going to have to put your IV back in and feed you intravenously."

He reached for the tray and started spooning soup in his mouth. "You do that, nurse, if it will help me regain my strength, because I'm getting out of here just as soon as I can."

She smiled her approval and left.

Steve ate ravenously, anxious to be released so he could try and find the one woman he knew beyond all doubt that he loved and wanted to marry.

And he couldn't allow her to go without letting her know that.

15

"**I** can't tell you anything, Miller," Chief Rogan said resolutely. "Casey had her own reasons for wanting everything kept confidential. I didn't ask what they were."

Steve argued, "But she was my partner, dammit. I have a right to know where she's gone."

"Why? She's not your partner anymore. She quit."

Steve had been sitting across from Rogan's desk for the past ten minutes begging, pleading, for information about Liz. He had reached the point where he didn't even care if the chief suspected his persistence was motivated by personal interest. All Steve knew was that he had reached the end of his rope in trying to find Liz. He'd gone to her apartment only to learn she had moved out and left no forwarding address. Her phone had been disconnected with no recording advising of a new number. He had even, in desperation, tried to call her father at the Montgomery Police Department but was told he and his wife were on vacation and wouldn't be back for two weeks.

Not giving up, Steve tried again to wheedle some clue from Rogan. "Just tell me if she's still in town or if she went someplace else. You can do that much, can't you?"

Rogan's expression was stony. "Sorry. No can do. Now look, let's get off the topic of Casey. She's history around here, and it's time for you to meet your new partner."

Steve shook his head. "Not yet, please. Give me a few more days, chief. I don't care what you say, I'm going to try and find Casey."

"Then go to it." Rogan got to his feet, signaling the meeting was over. "Do whatever you feel you have to do, and when you're ready—which I hope is soon—come on in and get back to work. I think you need to do that. I've never had the misfortune of being wounded, but I hear it helps to get back in the swing of things as soon as possible. Sort of like getting back on a horse after you've been thrown," he added in an attempt to lighten Steve's somber mood.

Steve left his office and went to the big room where each detective had a desk. Everyone was out, so he went to Casey's and went through it again. He had already found every drawer empty, but wanted to check one more time to see if she might have left some clue behind.

"Some detective you are, Miller," he admonished himself under his breath. "You can't even find your partner."

He knew, however, that eventually he would be able to do so. She would surface somewhere. He would find a new address for her car registration on computer, or he would go through the utility records for every town in the state of Alabama if he had to. But he didn't want to wait, because the more time that passed before he could explain everything, the more she would drift away from him, bitterness growing all the while.

And besides all that, he was miserable without her.

He decided to grill the supervisor, Mrs. Barnes, at the apartment complex again. He had been there already, and Mrs. Barnes had refused to be intimidated. He had even flashed his badge, but she had sneered and said she didn't give a fig if he were Dirty Harry himself. She didn't know where Liz had gone and wouldn't tell him if she did.

Steve couldn't help smiling, albeit bittersweetly, to hear the Dirty Harry bit. Liz had told him how she felt everyone compared detectives to the character.

He thought of her sense of humor and all the good times they'd had together and whispered, "Oh, God, I miss you," past the lump in his throat.

So he would try Mrs. Barnes again and was not above bribing her with a hundred-dollar bill if that's what it took. Maybe even more, because he had never known such desperation and longing in his life.

He was walking out of the office when a miracle happened—he recognized Carol Batson as she was walking in.

"Thank God. I'd forgotten about you," he cried, grabbing her by her shoulders.

For an instant she was frightened, then anger dropped over her face like a veil. Not thinking about him having been wounded and still recuperating, she popped him in his sides with the heels of her hands. "Let go of me, Miller, or I'll deck you, I swear."

He winced and dropped his hold. "Wait a minute. I didn't mean to come on so strong. I just want to ask you about Liz Casey. I remember seeing you two together at the Blue Spot."

"Yeah? So?" She gave her shoulder-length hair a toss and lifted her chin. "Well, I don't have time to talk to you now. I've got an appointment with Chief Rogan."

"It can wait. Please," he begged. "Tell me where she is. I've got to find her."

"Maybe she doesn't want you to."

"But I've got to. We had a misunderstanding, and I want to talk to her and try to straighten things out."

Carol, ever nosy, took advantage of his obviously vulnerable state and sweetly asked, "What kind of things, Miller? What did you do to upset her so?"

"I'd rather not say."

She snapped, "Then I don't know where she is."

He dared put a hand of camaraderie on her shoulder, and, for an instant thought she was going to whack his sides again but mercifully didn't. "Look, Batson. I've been a detective long enough to tell when somebody is trying to hide something."

"Really?" she asked brightly, brows raised. "Is it a special talent or can anybody learn to do it?"

"Don't be smart," he warned. "I don't have time."

"I'm not being smart—honest. I have a reason for wanting to know. You see—"

"I'm not interested in hearing it. Just tell me where she is."

Her chin jutted out again. "Why should I? She hates your guts, Miller, because you lied to her."

"I know I did," he admitted. "But I had my reasons, and I can only hope once she hears them, she'll understand why I did it."

"You lied about having a girlfriend back in California, didn't you? We met her, you know. She looks like Barbie."

"Barbie?" He shook his head. The conversation was going nowhere fast. "That woman was Marla Nivens, and she was never my girlfriend. She was the sister of the woman who was—only she's dead now. Marla came to tell me something important. That's all it was. Now are you going to help me find Liz so I can explain all this or not? I'll find her sooner or later, you know. But you can save me a lot of time."

"She'll be mad if I do."

"I won't tell her you did. Just give me a hint—anything to help me find her—and I'll pretend I tracked her down myself. What's the harm, Batson?"

"The harm," Batson retorted, eyes flashing, "is that you've hurt her enough. I don't want you to do it again."

He fixed her in his burning gaze as he tersely declared, "I will not hurt her, because I love her more than anything in this world, and I want a chance to tell her that."

Hearing that, Carol didn't take long to make up her mind. "She's going to school at Jefferson Tech. She gets out of class around nine. That's all I'm going to tell you."

She pulled from his grasp and hurried on by before he could ask any more questions.

Steve spent the rest of the day counting hours till nine o'clock. At eight he drove by Mulvaney's house and asked to borrow the cruiser. Mulvaney didn't ask why he wanted it, and Steve wouldn't have told him if he had asked.

Jefferson Tech was a county technical school offering a variety of vocational curricula, located on the outskirts of Birmingham towards Hueytown. Promptly at nine o'clock Steve was parked off to the side of the main road leading into the campus.

At 9:10 he spotted Liz's car and pulled in after her, hitting the cruiser's blue light.

She edged to the curb, but he didn't park behind her as he normally would have done were he legitimately stopping someone. Instead, he eased to the front to make it more difficult for her to drive away should she recognize him and be infuriated.

But it was dark, and she couldn't see his face.

"License and registration," he said crisply once he reached the open window on the driver's side.

"Show me your badge, first," she said tightly. "You aren't in uniform."

"I'm plainclothes, miss. Now are you going to show me your license and registration?"

It hit her then.

The voice.

Plainclothes.

She leaned out the window to look up at him in the glow from the interior lights and gasped, "Steve. How did you—"

"It doesn't matter how I found you," he leaned down so they were eye level. "But I had to, Liz. I had to tell you why I lied about California."

She placed both hands tightly on the steering wheel and stared straight ahead. "It doesn't matter."

"Yes, it does, because I love you and only you. Don't you know that?"

He saw her reach uncertainly for the ignition switch.

"Marla Nivens," he rushed to tell her, "is the sister of the woman who was my partner. She was killed one night when we were making a bust, and I blamed myself. That's why I left California, because I wanted to run from the past."

The rage Liz was fighting against exploded as she cried, "But it was *her* name—Marla's—that you called when I held you in my arms and told you how much I loved you."

"Then I wasn't dreaming." He smiled, despite how she looked at him in loathing and contempt. "I thought I heard you speaking to me, but I was in such a fog. All I could think about was how I wanted to tell you Marla meant nothing to me. That must be why I spoke her name."

Liz's hand fell from the switch, and she turned to look at him, lips quivering as she fought to keep from crying. "Why couldn't you have told me all this before, Steve?"

He shook his head in misery. "It was something I had to deal with in my own way, but I see now I should have told you when you first asked me about whether I had a girl back in California. Evidently somebody leaked something from personnel. It was in my file that my partner was killed.''

''Was that all she was to you, Steve? Your partner?''

''No,'' he said candidly, not about to lie to her again about anything. ''I thought I was in love with her. That's why I fought so hard to keep from loving you—because I swore I'd never get personally involved again with anyone I worked with.

''And after what happened in California,'' he went on to explain, ''I didn't want a female partner, either. So you were right when you accused me of trying to make you look incompetent, only, once I fell in love with you I wanted you with me.''

Tears were shimmering in Liz's eyes. ''Oh, Steve. If only you'd told me....''

''But I didn't, and I'm sorry. Can you forgive me?'' He cupped her chin in his hand as he drank in the sight of her beloved face. ''I love you, and I want us to be together.''

''As partners?'' She shook her head. ''I've changed careers, Steve. I'm going to be a parole officer. I've realized that's what I want to do.''

''And you'll make a hell of a good one, too,'' he said, pleased. ''But it wouldn't matter to me if you kept on working as a detective. I'd never try to tell you how to live your life, honey. Believe that.''

It was the words she had longed to hear...words she had begun to think a man would never say to her. Only now they meant even more, for she was hearing them from a man she had come to realize that she loved with all her heart.

She reached for him, stretching her arms out the window to draw him as close as possible, and kissed him until they were both breathless.

When he could, at last, bring himself to pull away, Steve

laughed shakily and said, "How about if we go someplace where we can talk? It's kind of awkward like this, and I want so much to hold you."

"I don't have a place anymore," she told him.

"I know. But *I* do, and Mamie has missed you, too."

"Then lead the way." She smiled from her heart, loving him, wanting him and knowing she would never, ever let him go.

He kissed her again and turned to walk away, but she couldn't resist teasing, "What about my ticket? Aren't you going to write me up?"

He whirled about to say, "The only ticket I have for you, sweetheart, is a ticket to the happiest future I've got in my power to give you.

"And that's the truth," he added with a grin.

Epilogue

———◄———

"I don't know why the chief insisted on seeing both of us," Steve said as he walked with Liz up the steps to the second floor of the precinct. "Especially on my first official day back, and you don't even work here anymore."

It had been nearly a month since Steve's release from the hospital, and he felt he was ready to get back to work.

Liz, clasping his hand, said, "Well, I had a lot to do today, but I always liked Rogan, and if he's got something he wants to say, I'll listen to it."

"And we both have an idea of what that's going to be."

"Exactly. He wants to let us know he is well aware that we were fraternizing when we were partners and go through the motions of giving us a slap on the wrist."

Steve held up her left hand, and her diamond ring glittered in the overhead light as they reached the landing outside the Detective Bureau. "He's heard about this. Everybody has. And I guess he's got sense enough to know it didn't happen overnight. So," he said with a sigh of resignation, "let's get it over with."

The door opened, and they were instantly greeted with shouts and cheers amidst a flutter of confetti and balloons.

Liz and Steve looked at each other, stunned to realize it was a surprise engagement party.

Everyone moved in to hug Liz and shake Steve's hand,

and then they were further astonished when Carol appeared. She was wearing a blazer, blouse and skirt, and had a big, mischievous grin pasted on her face.

"We fooled you, didn't we?" she bragged. "You never suspected a thing."

"No, we honestly didn't," Liz said, wondering why Carol was there, too, dressed like she was. "We thought Chief Rogan was going to chew us out for getting involved with each other when we were partners."

"I know," she giggled. "That's why we used that as an excuse to get you up here." She turned to Steve. "But he really does want to see you about something, when all the excitement dies down. You've got to cut the cake, and—"

"Miller. Casey. Congratulations." Rogan walked up to them. "So when is the big day?"

"Not till June," Liz answered. "My father is insisting on a big wedding for his baby girl."

"Wonderful, wonderful. I'll be there." He gave Steve a firm pat on his back. "And I see you've already met your partner."

Steve felt a sinking sensation at how Carol was grinning up at him so impishly. "You...you don't mean—"

"I sure do," Rogan confirmed. "We had a vacancy, and Batson had done so well in patrol that when she applied for the position, we were glad to bring her in."

Liz put her hand over her mouth to keep from exploding with laughter, while Steve groaned and slapped his forehead.

"He was going to tell you that first day you came in after you got out of the hospital," Carol said, beaming, "but that was also the day you made me tell you how to find Liz, remember?"

"I remember," Steve said. "Now will somebody please

tell me this is a nightmare, and I'll eventually wake up and it won't be happening?''

"Sorry," Carol gave him a playful clip on the jaw. "But it's me and you from now on...Dirty Harry."

She drifted away with Chief Rogan, and Liz turned to Steve to whisper, "No, she's wrong. It's *you* and *me* from now on."

"You've got that right," he grinned, pulling her into his arms. "And knowing that, I reckon there's nothing I can't handle."

And as they kissed, everyone broke into another round of cheers and applause.

"Cops 'n' kisses," the chief remarked with a smile as he stood watching. "Maybe it ain't so bad after all."

* * * * *

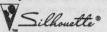

Take 2 bestselling love stories FREE

Plus get a FREE surprise gift!

Special Limited-Time Offer

Mail to Silhouette Reader Service™

3010 Walden Avenue
P.O. Box 1867
Buffalo, N.Y. 14269-1867

YES! Please send me 2 free Silhouette Yours Truly™ novels and my free surprise gift. Then send me 4 brand-new novels every other month, which I will receive months before they appear in bookstores. Bill me at the low price of $2.90 each plus 25¢ delivery and applicable sales tax, if any.* That's the complete price, and a saving of over 10% off the cover prices—quite a bargain! I understand that accepting the books and gift places me under no obligation ever to buy any books. I can always return a shipment and cancel at any time. Even if I never buy another book from Silhouette, the 2 free books and the surprise gift are mine to keep forever.

201 SEN CH72

Name	(PLEASE PRINT)	
Address	Apt. No.	
City	State	Zip

This offer is limited to one order per household and not valid to present Silhouette Yours Truly™ subscribers. *Terms and prices are subject to change without notice. Sales tax applicable in N.Y.

USYT-98   ©1996 Harlequin Enterprises Limited

MATERNITY LEAVE

Coming September 1998

Three delightful stories about the blessings
and surprises of "Labor" Day.

TABLOID BABY by Candace Camp

She was whisked to the hospital in the nick of time....

THE NINE-MONTH KNIGHT
by Cait London

A down-on-her-luck secretary is experiencing
odd little midnight cravings....

THE PATERNITY TEST by Sherryl Woods

The stick turned blue before her
biological clock struck twelve....

*These three special women are very pregnant...and very
single, although they won't be either for too much longer,
because baby—and Daddy—are on their way!*

Available at your favorite retail outlet.

MEN at WORK

All work and no play?
Not these men!

July 1998
MACKENZIE'S LADY by Dallas Schulze

Undercover agent Mackenzie Donahue's
lazy smile and deep blue eyes were his best
weapons. But after rescuing—and kissing!—
damsel in distress Holly Reynolds, how could
he betray her by spying on her brother?

August 1998
MISS LIZ'S PASSION by Sherryl Woods

Todd Lewis could put up a building with ease,
but quailed at the sight of a classroom! Still,
Liz Gentry, his son's teacher, was no battle-ax,
and soon Todd started planning some
extracurricular activities of his own....

September 1998
A CLASSIC ENCOUNTER
by Emilie Richards

Doctor Chris Matthews was intelligent, sexy
and *very* good with his hands—which made
him all the more dangerous to single mom
Lizette St. Hilaire. So how long could she
resist Chris's special brand of TLC?

Available at your favorite retail outlet!

MEN AT WORK™

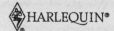

 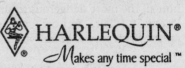

**Available September 1998
from Silhouette Books...**

World's Most
Eligible Bachelors

THE CATCH
OF CONARD COUNTY
by Rachel Lee

Rancher Jeff Cumberland: long, lean, sexy as sin. He's eluded every marriage-minded female in the county. Until a mysterious woman breezes into town and brings her fierce passion to his bed. Will this steamy Conard County courtship take September's hottest bachelor off of the singles market?

Each month, Silhouette Books brings you an irresistible bachelor in these all-new, original stories. Find out how the sexiest, most sought-after men are finally caught...

Available at your favorite retail outlet.

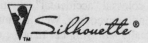

Silhouette®

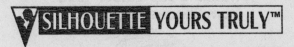

SILHOUETTE YOURS TRULY™

*Sneak Previews of October titles
from Yours Truly™:*

THE BAD-GIRL BRIDE
by Jennifer Drew

Nice girls finish last! So jilted Julie Myers was looking for
My-Fair-Lady lessons—in reverse! 'Cause to attract *more*
men, she figured she had to become a little *less* of a lady.
And she found the perfect instructor in rogue
Tom Brunswick. Trouble was, Tom's Habits for Highly
Effective Matchmaking were, uh, highly effective. And
while she could suddenly have her pick of handsome men,
she'd gone and fallen for the reigning expert on seduce-
and-resist—her teacher! While Tom was busy changing
Julie's good-girl image, had *she* somehow changed this
bad boy's mind about marriage?

THE ACCIDENTAL FIANCÉ
Women To Watch
by Krista Thoren

Gorgeous Grant Addison and strong-willed
Brianna Tully had to either pretend to be happily,
exclusively dating…or send their do-gooder sisters to
Matchmakers Anonymous! But that put-on gleam in
her eyes and that make-believe desire in his were too good
to be *false*…which fired up the family rumor mill and
sparked the colossal "accidental" announcement of
their impending wedding. Well, Brianna had no
intention of actually *marrying* her fiancé…even though he
secretly intended to make his mistaken bride-to-be
his real-life wife!